High on a Hill

*Also by Frances Y. McHugh
in Large Print:*

Emerald Mountain

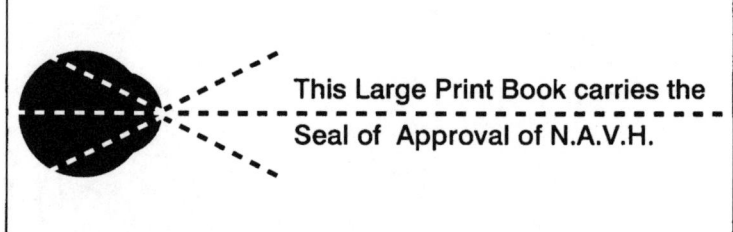

High on a Hill

Frances Y. McHugh

G.K. Hall & Co. • Thorndike, Maine

Copyright © 1967, by Arcadia House

All rights reserved.

Published in 2000 by arrangement with Maureen Moran Agency

G.K. Hall Large Print Paperback Series.

The text of this Large Print edition is unabridged.
Other aspects of the book may vary from the original edition.

Set in 16 pt. Plantin Warren S. Doersam.

Printed in the United States on permanent paper.

Library of Congress Cataloging-in-Publication Data

McHugh, Frances Y.
    High on a hill / by Frances Y. McHugh.
       p. cm.
    ISBN 0-7838-8938-0 (lg. print : sc : alk. paper)
    1. Americans — Travel — France — Fiction. 2. Large type books.
 I. Title.
PS3563.C3685 H54   2000
813'.54—dc21   99-058078

High on a Hill

Chapter One

I had been told the château I was going to was high on a hill, but no one had mentioned the fact that it was a veritable castle.

My first glimpse of it was from the train window as I sat waiting for the porter to come for my bags. In the distance I could see one of those little hill towns so prevalent in southern France, with the red-tiled roofs of small houses snuggled around the bottom of the hill and a scattered few staggering up to the wall that always surrounded the château on the top; remnants of feudal days.

The name of the town was *Fleur-sur-Mer*. Flower-on-the-sea. It was about ten miles west of Nice, which I looked forward to seeing, if I ever got away long enough from my responsibilities in the château on the hill.

As the train had sped through the countryside from Paris, down to Marseilles and across the *Côte d'Azur* toward Nice, I had plenty of time to think. I decided I had done all the wrong things.

It had all started two years ago when Mark Preston first came to the Graylock Advertising Agency. He had been a nice, clean-cut, eager young man just out of college. I'd thought he was the best-looking man I'd ever seen. He was tall, blond, with a straight military carriage and a nice pair of shoulders. And very smart. He was also ambitious. But very inexperienced in the ways of the business world.

And so I had taken him in hand. As secretary to Mr. Hobart Graylock, president of the agency, I was in a position to know what was what, and what Mr. Graylock expected of his junior copy writers and potential junior account executives.

Mark had sensed this and made it a point always to ask my advise before he made a move. He would come into my small private office that connected with Mr. Graylock's larger, luxurious office and sit on the side of my desk and say, "Carol, honey, have you time to read this piece of copy?" And I would say, "Of course," and stop what I was doing and read the copy he had written and make suggestions as to how it could be changed to conform more nearly to Mr. Graylock's views on copywriting. Mark had a flair for it. He had taken some chemistry in college, and as most of our clients were pharmaceutical houses, he was perfect for the job.

After a while I found myself inviting him to my apartment for little dinners for two, after which we would have long talks about life and how to succeed in a big city.

I was three years older than he, so I guess I felt a little superior, and the fact that I had survived alone in the big city for the last three years, ever since I graduated from college and my parents had died in a plane crash, was proof that I knew what I was talking about.

Mark was from a small town in Ohio and had gone to a small college. His family were farmers, not rich, not poor. But one time he had confided in me that when he got to college he discovered, to his dismay, that his clothes were all wrong. What he had thought to be high style turned out to be just loud and in bad taste. It had taken him his entire freshman year to dispose gradually of the wrong pieces of clothing and replace them with the kind of things the other fellows were wearing. And rather than tell his folks his predicament, he had gotten odd jobs around town during his leisure hours and earned the money for the new and more suitable things, which, I thought, was very commendable. It had taken me several months to get up enough courage to tell him that some of his things were still wrong. When I finally did, he was most grateful and kissed me for the first time in other than just a casual, friendly manner.

From then on, things had moved swiftly, both for Mark and for me. For me it had been a whirlwind courtship which took my breath away. Of course I had had men friends before Mark, but never had I felt toward any of them the way I felt toward him. For Mark, it had been a jet-propelled rise to the top of the ladder in the agency.

I had wanted him to succeed and had subtly and gently taught him the right things to do: in conferences with clients; at lunch and dinner with clients; when he was invited to the boss's house for dinner. He became the best dressed man in the agency. He became the boss's liaison between himself and their most important clients. His good looks and inherent charm, along with the things I'd taught him, catapulted him to the top so fast he no longer had time for chats or little dinners for two with Carol Benson, the boss's efficient secretary. And what had gradually become an unspoken and unofficial engagement between him and me had as gradually become a big nothing. Only by that time I had fallen deeply in love with him.

In the beginning I had too much pride to have a showdown with the man who was now the fair-haired boy of the agency. I was proud of him. I admired him. And I loved him. But if he was too busy and too involved to bother with me any more, then that was it, as far as I was concerned. Besides, lately he had been going to the Graylocks' big house out on Long Island more and more frequently. And he was beginning to be mentioned in the society columns as Gloria Graylock's "latest."

That did it! Gloria had a reputation for picking men up and dropping them as casually as if they were pebbles on a beach. But Mark didn't know that, or if he did he didn't let it bother him. Then one day I exploded and demanded to know where I stood.

He looked surprised. "I don't understand

what you mean," he said.

"You don't? Well, then, I'll explain." I knew I was going about it all wrong. But I couldn't help it. I was desperate. I looked up into his big brown eyes and saw nothing in them but a complete disregard for myself. "What I mean is — I thought we were friends; even more: sweethearts."

He smiled and raised an eyebrow, one of his latest tricks. "Well, we *are* friends," he said.

"But no longer sweethearts?"

The corners of his mouth tightened. "I suppose what you are getting at is that you have seen my name coupled with Gloria Graylock's in the papers lately?"

I nodded. "Is it serious?"

He was sitting on the side of my desk and Mr. Graylock was out, so we were alone. He began to swing one leg, and as he did so he watched the toe of his expensive, highly polished shoe. "I suppose you won't be able to understand this," he said, "but security means a lot to me."

I watched his handsome face. Tiny lines were beginning to show in his forehead and on either side of his mouth, as if he were under a continual strain. I hadn't noticed before. "You mean *financial* security?" I asked.

He took his gaze from his shoe and turned it on me. "What other kind is there?" His eyes were wide with surprise.

"Well, silly as it may sound, there is *emotional* security."

He smiled. "You surprise me," he said, "even

disappoint me. I should think a big city girl like you would know that financial security practically guarantees emotional security."

"Does it?"

"Doesn't it?"

"Then are you planning on marrying Gloria Graylock?"

He smiled. He had nice even white teeth. "It's an idea I've had under consideration."

"And it would give you security?"

His smile broadened. "Wouldn't it? If I was married to the boss's daughter, I couldn't be fired."

"Had you that in mind when you first joined the agency?"

He slid to his feet and rammed his hands into his trouser pockets. "When I first came here I wouldn't have had a chance."

Many accusations rushed to my trembling lips, but I tightened them so none of the cutting remarks could escape.

He stood watching me for a few moments, then said, "I know what you're thinking. You're thinking about all the help you've given me; teaching me how to dress, how to behave, how to be a — well, a success."

I looked out the window and watched a pigeon strut across the hill. I didn't speak because there was such an ache in my throat I couldn't. So he said, "And you are right. You *have* made me what I am today — a success. And I *am* grateful. Thank you."

That was all. He turned and walked out of the office.

So that was that. Only I didn't have to sit there and take it. Thank heaven I had a stock certificate left to me by my grandmother that would sell on the present market for around two thousand dollars.

All the self-betterment books I had ever read said that if your life was in a mess, you should do something about it. In other words: pick yourself up, dust yourself off, and start all over again. Well, that was exactly what I intended to do. It was almost spring, and I'd always wanted to be in Paris in the springtime. So why not now?

I hated to give up my good job at the agency, but I knew I couldn't stay without being miserable. So I sold my stock and started the wheels turning that would take me to Paris, away from it all. I bought my plane ticket, applied for my passport, had my shots. And all through it I avoided Mark.

I made no mention of my plans in the office. When everything was settled I would give Mr. Graylock two weeks' notice and sublet my apartment, saying I felt I needed a change. When I came back I'd look for a job somewhere else and get a new apartment.

In the meantime, Gloria's and Mark's engagement was announced. I tried to leave New York before the wedding, but couldn't make it; they were married a week before I was scheduled to leave. The honeymoon plans had been kept secret, so even I, secretary to Gloria's father, didn't know where they were going. And of course I didn't go to the wedding, even though I was invited.

And then, my very first day in Paris, what did I do but bump smack bang into Mark on the *Rue Royale!* He was wearing a light gray suit and looked stunning. My heart quavered, and for a moment the old feeling for him engulfed me. "Mark!" I cried, and automatically my hands went out to him. Mark gripped my hand and looked down into my eyes. "Carol," he cried, "what on earth are you doing in Paris?"

"Taking a little vacation."

He kept hold of my hands. "I couldn't believe it when H.G. told me you'd resigned."

I pulled away my hands. "What was I supposed to do? Sit there and watch you make a fool of yourself?"

His face sobered. "I'm sorry, Carol," he said. "It was just one of those things."

"Precisely," I said, and turned away.

But he grabbed my arm. "Wait! Don't run away from me like that." Holding me so I couldn't get away, he said, "Forget the whole thing, and let's have some fun."

I pulled my arm from his grasp. "Fun? With me? Where is Gloria?" My first feeling of gladness at seeing him collapsed and disintegrated like something that had been hit by a ray from a laser gun. I watched his face tighten. "Oh, yes, Gloria," he said. "She's shopping. Buying clothes and more clothes."

I stared up at him. "I didn't know you and Gloria were coming to Paris on your honeymoon," I said. "Or . . ."

He smiled. "Or you wouldn't have come here. Or would you?"

The implication of that made my face flush. "Really, Mark, you are impossible!" I said crossly.

He stopped smiling. "I'm a fool!" he said. "And I have made a terrible mistake. I should never have married Gloria."

A chill ran down my back. "But you are on your honeymoon. You've only been married a week. How can you talk like that?"

He shrugged. "Easy. The bare truth of the matter is that I am just a gigolo."

"Stop feeling sorry for yourself," I told him, and for the first time since I'd known him I saw him as he really was. "You wanted security — financial security — and now you have it."

"Yes, I have it. But I don't have any freedom. I can't even say my soul is my own. My honeymoon was planned for me, and paid for by Poppa. We are going to spend it at Poppa's château down on the Riviera. We are just passing through Paris so Gloria can shop and throw a few parties. And when we get back to the States, Poppa is buying us a house near him on the Island, furnishing it, and putting a car in the garage for us; maybe two, one for each of us."

"But that's wonderful!" I said, thinking that I would hate to have someone else select my house, furniture and car.

"Wonderful? It is?" Mark asked.

"Well, it is exactly what you wanted. It's security with a capital S."

"It's slavery with a capital S," Mark said bitterly.

I didn't know what to say. This was a new Mark, one I neither knew nor liked. "Well, it's nice to see you," I said quickly. "I have to go now." I turned to cross the street, but again he grabbed my arm. "Wait! What are you doing this evening?"

I looked him directly in the eyes. "What is your wife doing?"

His lip curled. "Oh, she's throwing a big party in our suite at the *Crillon*. But after an hour or so it will be such a rat race no one will miss me if I slip out, least of all her. Oh yes, Poppa arrived this morning. I forgot to tell you that."

"But you are on your honeymoon," I reminded again. "Of course your wife will miss you. She is in love with you. Why else would she have married you?"

He shrugged. "Love? If she knows the meaning of the word, she is keeping it a secret, from *me* anyway. And besides, I have a feeling that I am being used. Being married to me is a convenience for her — or for Poppa."

I touched his hand gently. "I'm sorry, Mark," I said. "But I'm sure it will turn out all right. Perhaps you should work a little harder at being a husband."

He looked down into my eyes and sighed. "Would you come to the party tonight? Just for a few minutes? You're smart. If you could see us together, perhaps you'd see — well, more than I have been able to see so far. To tell you the truth, I'm confused about the whole thing."

"I couldn't do that," I said.

"Why not?"

"Well, for one thing, I haven't been invited. Besides, I don't know Gloria very well. She might not want me."

"She wouldn't care. She knew about you and me, but it didn't make any difference to her."

I hesitated.

"Please come," he said. "I feel I owe it to you to give you a chance to gloat."

"You know I'd never do that."

His smile was crooked as he said, "Security, thou art a traitor! Besides, I am a husband in name only. And that should be good for at least one laugh — from you." Then he walked away.

As I hurried along I tried to feel elated because Mark had gotten exactly what he deserved. But retribution never is any comfort to the one who has been wronged. And I knew that in spite of myself, I was going to attend that party at the *Crillon* that evening.

Chapter Two

Perhaps I shouldn't have gone to the party on the strength of just Mark's invitation, but something stronger than myself seemed to be pushing me into it. So after a lonely dinner in the dining room of my small hotel back of the *Madeleine*, I went up to my room and dressed very carefully.

I had no idea what kind of clothes would be worn to a party of that sort in a private suite at the *Hotel Crillon* in Paris, but when I had shopped for this trip I had splurged a little, so I had a good selection of dresses to choose from.

I decided on a pale green silk sleeveless shift which ended a couple of inches above my knees with a full ruffle. I had never had the courage to wear anything like a mini-skirt in New York, but when I shopped for clothes to wear in Paris, I took the bull by the horns and decided to give my knees a chance to see the sights. They are nice-looking knees, as knees go, so what the heck. And green is a good color for me, because my hair is a dark auburn and my light brown eyes have a slightly-greenish cast.

In the office I had always worn my hair, which is quite thick, in a neat bun. But for the party I decided I'd let it hang loose in what is known as "a fall," with a green ribbon tied around my head to keep it back from my face. I'd worn it that way sometimes when Mark had come to my apartment to dinner, and he liked it. I had high-heeled green sandals and a short white fur cape. Not mink, but dyed something or other which, for me, answered the purpose.

I could have walked to the *Crillon* from my hotel, but decided that was no way to arrive at a place like that. So I took a taxi.

When I entered the lobby I went to the desk to ask for . . . Suddenly I didn't know whom to ask for. Was the suite taken in the name of Graylock or Preston? Well, it should be in the name of Preston. So I asked for Madame Mark Preston. For a moment the clerk looked puzzled; then suddenly he smiled. *"Ah oui,"* he said, *"Mademoiselle Gloria Graylock,"* and gave me the number of their suite.

I walked over to the elevator and entered with several other people who, I discovered, were going to the same place I was.

I was glad to see the girls were dressed similarly to myself. One man had on a dark business suit and one a tuxedo. There were even a couple of beatniks with long hair and sloppy clothes. I wondered if they were artists.

One man in particular stood out from the rest. He was tall, dark and very nice-looking, with the élite air of the sophisticated French gentleman. He had a close-cropped black moustache and steel gray eyes, and he held his well shaped head above the crowd in a way that suggested he was with it, but not of it. He had on a perfectly fitting dark blue business suit, a white shirt and a dark maroon tie. No hat, so I could see his hair had a slight wave. For a moment our eyes met, and I felt as if his could see right into my mind and read my every thought. Quickly I looked away, but I couldn't help being curious about him. Who was he? Was he a client of one of the Graylock foreign offices? Or was he one of Gloria's personal friends? Whoever he was, I had the feeling he was somebody special.

The Graylock suite seemed to cover considerable space. Double doors which were wide open showed a large entrance hall, filled with people, and beyond this was a large drawing room, also milling with people.

I hesitated at the door, wondering what I should do. There was no one there to receive guests. So I watched to see what the people who came up on the elevator with me did. They went to a cloak room at the side of the entrance hall and left their wraps. So I did the same. Then I sauntered into the large room behind them. But there again I was at a loss. I had deliberately come late so the party would be in full swing when I arrived, and it surely was. Everybody was talking and laughing and had a drink in his or her hand. The Frenchman said something to the cloak room attendant, then disappeared through a door across the hall.

There were several languages being spoken,

but mostly French. English came to me from various groups, and there was a smattering of Italian and Spanish and even German. Very cosmopolitan, I decided.

Then I saw Mark. He was wearing a new tuxedo, and I had never seen him look so attractive. With his usual charm and *savoir faire,* he was wandering about among the guests, greeting them graciously and being the perfect host. He was the only one in the room who did not have a drink in his hand, and from his behavior I could tell he hadn't had one. For a fleeting moment I was proud of him. He'd made the grade, and he was acting the part perfectly. I waited until he saw me standing in the doorway. He smiled and raised a hand in greeting; then, excusing himself to a group of people, he hurried over to me. "Carol!" he cried. "You came. I'm glad." He held out a hand to me and pulled me into the crowded room. "Let me get you a drink," he said. "Over here. There's a bar set up." I didn't want a drink, but it would give me a chance to quiet the feeling of excitement which was welling up in me. Looking around, I could not see Gloria or her father. I asked Mark, "Where is your wife?"

He looked down at me and shrugged. "My wife? Well, I don't know exactly at the moment. Does it matter?"

"Yes. I'd like to see her, wish her happiness in her marriage."

He stopped and let go of my hand. "You're

kidding, of course."

I began to feel angry. "No, I am not!" I told him. "Or if your wife isn't around, where is Mr. Graylock? I'd like to see him."

He gave me a wink. "Want to ask for your job back?"

"Certainly not."

Just then, before we'd reached the bar, I saw Mr. Graylock come out of a door on the far side of the room. For a moment he looked around. When he saw Mark he strode over to him. I thought he looked worried. He was rather a homely man, with large features, and had grown heavier since I'd first gone to work for him three years before.

When he reached Mark he said, "Can I see you a minute, boy? It's Gloria. She's not feeling well."

Then he recognized me, and I thought the tense lines in his face relaxed somewhat. "Oh, Carol," he said, "I didn't know you were coming to Paris."

"I didn't tell anybody."

He looked at me for a moment, and there was approval in his eyes. "You are different, aren't you?"

I smiled. "You mean from the way I used to look in the office?"

"Well, yes. But whatever it is, I like it."

I said, "Thank you."

He stood looking at me for a moment; then he said, "Would you do something for me, Carol?"

It was almost a plea.

"If I can." He had felt badly when I'd handed in my resignation and had given me a hundred-dollar-gift certificate to Saks Fifth Avenue as a goodbye present, so I felt I would like to help him if I could.

"Come with me," he said.

While Mr. Graylock had been talking to me, Mark had wandered off to join a group of people on the other side of the room.

As I followed Mr. Graylock, I asked, "Do you want Mark?"

He glanced around the room, located his son-in-law and said, "No. It doesn't matter," and led me through the door from which I'd seen him come a few minutes before. It led into a small reception hall, then into a suite of rooms that could have been a royal suite. A large, beautifully furnished living room was empty except for two people; a girl who was sprawled on one of the couches which flanked the empty fireplace, and a man. The girl was Gloria, her white gold hair spread over a light blue brocade pillow, her pretty face pale and her heavily shadowed lids closed over what I knew were greenish blue eyes. Standing looking down at her was the tall, dark, distinguished Frenchman who had come up in the elevator with me. When Mr. Graylock saw him, he stopped, his face going chalk white. "How did *you* get in here?" he demanded.

The Frenchman quirked up one dark eyebrow. "I know my way around this hotel," he said. "There is a back door to this suite."

"Well, get out. And stay out. And keep away from my daughter. I thought you were down in South America."

"I came back." The man looked down at the unconscious girl. "She is still very beautiful," he said softly. *"Ma chérie."*

"She is not your *chérie!*" Mr. Graylock snapped, advancing toward him. "And if you don't keep away from her, I'll have you arrested!"

The man turned and looked at him, and although they were the same height he gave the impression of looking down upon the older man. "I think not," he said quietly. Then, almost in one motion, he bowed politely to Mr. Graylock, leaned down and kissed Gloria on the forehead. Before Mr. Graylock could say anything more, he said, *"Au revoir,"* and walked out of the room the way we had entered. There was a faint smile on his lips, and as his steel gray eyes looked at me in passing I had the feeling he would not quickly forget my face.

Mr. Graylock shook his head, he nodded to his daughter and said, "She's passed out."

I went over to her and touched one of her hands. It was like ice. "Maybe you should call a doctor?" I suggested.

He pulled over a gilt Louis XIV chair and sat down beside his daughter. "No," he said. "I know what is the matter with her."

Feeling very inadequate, I asked, "Too much party?"

He shook his head. "That is only part of it."

I stood beside the father and daughter, not knowing what to say or do. Finally Mr. Graylock said, "Too many sleeping pills. They don't mix well with liquor."

"Is there anything I can do?"

He sighed and looked up at me thoughtfully. "There is, but I hate to ask it of you."

"What is it?" I began to wish I wasn't there.

"Go down to the Riviera with her. Keep an eye on her until I can get my sister, her Aunt Veronica, over to take care of her."

"Can't Mark look after her?"

His broad thick shoulders sagged. "No. Mark doesn't know his way around here. To tell the truth, Mark is a disappointment." He put his hands up to his face and rubbed it vigorously. It was a habit he had when things weren't going right.

As I'd so often done in the office when he did that, I put a hand on his shoulder. I knew I didn't have to say anything. He would be all right in a few minutes. And he was. His hands dropped from his face, and he heaved a big sigh. "Gloria is the kind of a person who can't face reality," he said wearily.

Naturally the thought went through my mind that Gloria had never had to face reality. Even when her mother died, the blow was softened for her by her father and her aunt. And she had never had to go out and get a job and work for a living.

"Maybe she has had things too easy," I said. It was a thing I would never have dared to say while I was still working for him.

He gazed down at the lax face of his daughter. "Maybe." Then he looked up at me beseechingly. "If you will go down south with her, I'll pay you whatever you want."

"I'm sorry," I said. "I couldn't do that."

"Why not?" he demanded. Then, more pleasantly, "I know you're here on a little vacation, but it wouldn't be for long. My sister has a bad cold; it will take her a few days to feel well enough to travel. But she should be able to fly over in about a week or so, and then you could return to Paris and continue your — well, whatever you are planning on doing here."

I shook my head. "No," I said. "I'd rather not. Besides, I think Gloria would resent me trying to manage her. And I wouldn't know what to do. Perhaps you need a trained nurse."

I saw his eyes change. They became expressionless, the way they did when he was trying to put over a deal in the office and didn't want his opponent to know what he was up to. "No," he snapped. "It would be all over Europe in no time. I must think of the reputation of the agency."

I met his eyes boldly, and I knew there was defiance in mine. It was the first time I had ever defied him, and it took him by surprise. "Isn't your daughter's health and well-being more important?" I asked him. "If the girl is sick, she needs medical help, perhaps psychiatric help. Besides, her husband will be with her. He really is a nice boy."

He kept watching my face. "You used to be a very good friend of his, didn't you?"

"Yes."

He smiled ever so faintly. "You did a lot for him," he said. "You didn't think I noticed, but I did. And I thought your work had turned him into the kind of a fellow I needed — for Gloria. But . . ." He shrugged. "I guess he still needs you."

I backed away from him. "It's too late for that," I said, and started for the door.

"Wait!" he snapped at me.

I hesitated, so used was I to taking his orders. "What is your price?" he asked.

I'm afraid I glared at him. "I have no price, Mr. Graylock," I said. "And now good night." I hurried out of the room, out of the suite, through the now thinning crowd in the larger room and its entrance hall. I didn't even look to see where Mark was. I did, however surreptitiously glance around for the distinguished-looking Frenchman, but I didn't see him.

When I got back to my hotel room, I sat down and cried.

Chapter Three

The next two weeks were miserable for me. I wandered around Paris like a lost soul. I was contemplating returning to New York, feeling even worse than I had when I'd left it, when one day I met Mr. Graylock on the *Rue Seint Honoré*. "Carol!" he cried. "I've been trying to locate you. Have lunch with me."

The last thing I wanted to do was to lunch with Mr. Graylock, but I was so glad to see a familiar face, even if it did belong to Mark's father-in-law, that I let him take me to a quiet, expensive place on the *Boulevard des Italians*. As soon as we'd ordered he got right to the point. "You've got to go down to the Riviera," he said. "It's serious. I need your help."

I gulped half of my cinzano. "But didn't your sister come over?"

"Yes. But she can't manage alone. Besides, there are complications."

"What kind of complications?" I asked.

He toyed with his glass. He was drinking pernod. "I'm afraid I can't explain that," he said. "As a matter of fact, that is one reason I want you to go down. I want you to see if you can find out what is going on."

"But what *could* be going on?" I asked.

He shrugged. "I don't know. I'm baffled. And I'm worried about Gloria. She's worse over here than she was at home."

"Isn't Mark there with her?"

"Yes, but that hasn't helped any. They don't seem to get along."

I watched his face. He was plainly very worried about something. And after all, there wasn't anything to keep me in Paris. And if something was wrong down at the château, perhaps I could help not only Gloria, but Mark as well. As long as he'd gotten himself into this marriage, I would like to see him make a success of it. Fool that I was, I had always wanted Mark to be a success. Even now, at whatever cost to myself.

And Mr. Graylock had always been nice to me; it wouldn't hurt me to do him a favor, if I could. I asked, "How long would you want me to stay down south?"

His face brightened. "You mean you'll go?"

"If it will help any," I said, and gulped the rest of my cinzano.

Mr. Graylock heaved a deep sigh of relief. "I can't tell you how much I appreciate this," he said. "Can you leave tonight?"

I shrugged. "I suppose so."

He took my hand that was laying on the table. "Now I want to pay you something for this, Carol," he said. "Can't we make some kind of an arrangement?"

I didn't know what to say. Finally I suggested,

"Well, why don't you just pay me the same salary you did when I was in the office?"

He patted my hand. "Fine," he said. "We'll do it that way."

The waiter brought our soup and took away our empty *apéritif* glasses, and as soon as we were alone again Mr. Graylock said, "I want you to keep your eyes and ears open when you get down there and keep in close touch with me. I'm flying back to New York tonight. But don't hesitate to cable or even call me, reversing the charges."

"But what am I supposed to discover? I don't want to spy on Gloria. I couldn't do that."

"It's not a case of spying," he said. "It — well, it may be a case of saving her life."

And so now here I was on the Riviera.

The train was coming to a stop, and I got up, took my bags from the rack and staggered out of the compartment into the side corridor. There were a few other people also waiting to get off the train at *Fleur-sur-Mer,* and we all stood patiently until the train came to a stop.

As I started down the steps, a porter took my bags and said, *"Venez avec moi, mademoiselle."*

I followed him across the platform and was surprised to see him put my bags into the trunk of a white Mercedes-Benz sports car. When I started to tip him, a man appeared, seemingly from nowhere, and said, "I'll take care of it." I looked up — into the steel gray eyes of the Frenchman I'd seen at the Graylock party in

Paris. But today, in the bright Mediterranean sunshine, he didn't look quite so overpowering. He smiled. The sun in his eyes made them sparkle, and the gray was less steely. His teeth were very white, and even beneath his small black moustache he had nice firm lips. He was wearing sports clothes, and he still looked every inch the gentleman, but a more relaxed one. He said, "I thought it best that I meet you rather than one of the servants. At least you have seen me before."

I felt as if I'd been suddenly frozen. What was I getting into? Who was this man? How had he known I was arriving on this train?

He took my arm and led me to the car, opened the door and helped me into the passenger seat, closed the door, walked around and got into the driver's seat. He didn't speak until he'd turned the car onto a narrow and very steep road. Then he said, "This isn't really an automobile road. As a matter of fact, there isn't one that leads up to the top of the hill. Most people leave their cars down in the town and walk up. But occasionally a car can go up, if it goes very slowly." He spoke very good English with a slight British accent.

I looked around me. There were small houses on either side of the road, and there were no sidewalks; just concrete gutters on either side of the road.

Occasionally we would pass a pedestrian. Once it was a woman with a huge bundle of twigs balanced on her head. Farther up we had to pull over to the side to let a boy with a donkey cart pass by. The man I was with and the boy exchanged a few words in French, and the man tossed him a coin.

Halfway up I noticed the delicious smell of baking bread, and we passed a house with a sign *Epicerie* over the door. Standing in the doorway was a thick-set woman in a black dress with her hands on her hips. She had very red cheeks, like ripe apples. As we drove past, my companion lifted a hand in greeting to her. She nodded and said, *"Bon jour, monsieur dame."* Being included in her greeting, I nodded and turned and smiled.

My companion said, "That is *Madame Linard*. She mothers the whole town."

We finally reached the top of the hill, where there was a good-sized open space with a round fountain in the center. A girl was filling a pottery jug with water from the perpetually running fountain. There was no grass or sidewalks; just cobblestones for a pavement. "This is the *Place*," my companion said.

He guided the car through a stone archway and around a circular driveway bordered with bright-colored flowers and stopped before a large stone castle-like building. I supposed it was the château. *"Nous sommes arrives,"* he said, but he didn't make any attempt to get out of the car. He honked the horn, and in a moment one of the heavy wooden doors to the château was opened, and a man in a black suit and a red and white striped apron came out. My companion said,

"*Mademoiselle*'s bags are in the trunk of the car, *Jacques.*"

The man said, *"Oui, Monsieur Thireau."* It was the first time I had heard his name.

To me, *Jacques* said, *"Les dames* are expecting you, *mademoiselle.*"

I hesitated, not knowing what to do. Then I asked *Monsieur Thireau,* "Aren't you coming in?"

He said rather grimly, I thought, "No. From here on you are on your own."

It was a strange situation. "You do not stay here?" I asked him.

"No. You had better get out and go in." By then the man servant had taken my bags and gone into the house.

My companion leaned across me and opened the door on my side of the car. I got out, then turned to him and said, "Well, thank you, *monsieur,* for bringing me up. And incidentally, I am Carol Benson."

He nodded. "I know who you are, *mademoiselle.*"

I closed the door. He waited until I had walked around the front of the car and up to the open door of the château; then he started the car and drove it slowly around, out through the stone arch and around the fountain in the *Place.* The girl getting water at the fountain gave him a come-hither smile, but he didn't seem to notice.

I went up the stone steps and into the château, not knowing what to expect. After the bright sunshine outside, it was difficult for me to see in the dimness of the entrance, so I stood still for a moment. I could hear water trickling nearby, and the inside air felt very cool. When my eyes became accustomed to the change of light, I could see an elongated fountain, almost like a trough, with water trickling from a jar held by a stone nymph. At either side of the fountain a few steps went up to a large oblong hall furnished like a lounge in a club. I went up the steps to the right, and as I reached the top step Gloria came from a large room at my left. She was wearing sky blue slacks and a white turtle-necked sweater, with *espadrilles* on her bare feet. Her silver blonde hair was tied back from her face by a blue ribbon bow. She was very pale, and her blue eyes were enormous, with dark circles beneath them. She didn't seem to be too steady on her feet. She said, "So you really did come. I didn't think you would."

I walked over to her. She was a couple of inches shorter than my five foot seven, and very thin. "I hope you don't mind my coming," I said.

She shrugged and turned to go into the large room behind her, swayed alarmingly, and I grabbed her arm to keep her from falling. "What's the difference?" she asked me as I guided her over to a sofa and helped her to sit down. "Somebody has to watch me — why not you? Aunt Veronica gets tired of me."

"I don't understand," I said. "Why does

someone have to watch you?"

She smiled, resting her head on the back of the sofa. "I'm a naughty girl," she said, turning so she could look at me. "Didn't you know?"

"In what way?" I asked, feeling the chill of the room through my green linen suit.

She closed her eyes. "You'll find out," she said wearily.

Just then Aunt Veronica Meyerhoff came into the room, beautifully coiffed and dressed in a smart gray linen shift with colorful peasant embroidery around the neck and sleeves and a wide band of it at the bottom. She wore varicolored opera pumps and very sheer stockings. I remembered seeing shoes like that in a Fifth Avenue window and wishing I could have a pair, but they were way out of my price range. Although she was a woman of around fifty, Aunt Veronica had a slim, trim figure. "Is she talking nonsense again?" she asked me rather crossly. "Just don't pay any attention to her. Come; I'll show you to your rooms. *Jacques* has taken your bags up."

She led me toward the back of the lounge and up a wide, softly carpeted stairway to a balcony which had what looked like a hand-carved railing, a continuation of the stairway balustrade. Turning to the right, she led me down a long hallway, from which rooms opened on both sides. Some of the doors were closed and some weren't. Through the opened doors I could see beautifully furnished bedrooms.

The room she led me into was at the end of the hall. It was large and beautifully furnished in French provincial, with full-length windows opening onto a stone balcony which overlooked the Mediterranean. For a moment I could only stand and stare, it was so lovely. When I could speak, I said, "It's beautiful!"

Aunt Veronica turned and surveyed me with what I felt was a patronizing smile. "We want you to be comfortable," she said.

I saw my bags had been placed on folding stands at the foot of the large canopied bed. Aunt Veronica said, "I hope you don't mind unpacking for yourself. We are rather short of servants here."

I said, "No, of course not. I'm used to doing for myself."

She walked across the room to a door at the side. "This is your bathroom," she said. Then she smiled. "The natives hate us for modernizing these old places. They think we are spoiling their town."

I went over and looked into the bathroom. It wasn't very large, but it was very ornate; pink, with baroque gilt fixtures. Or they could have been gold, for all I knew.

Aunt Veronica went to the hall door. "Lunch will be in about half an hour," she said. "We will have it on the back terrace. We don't have a view of the sea from there, but we have a nice view of the Swiss alps in the distance and can see far over the countryside."

I said, "Thank you. I'll be down as soon as I freshen up."

The woman said, "Take your time." Then she looked at me speculatively before saying, "I don't know how much my brother has told you about Gloria's illness, but don't believe everything she says. She has hallucinations at times."

I drew in my breath, met her eyes and discovered they were almost black, which contrasted strongly with her blue-tinted white hair. In spite of myself I had to ask, "Where is her husband?"

"You mean Mark Preston?"

"Yes."

She shrugged. "My brother sent him back to New York. He left last night."

"But . . ."

She interrupted me. "Don't worry about it," she told me. "He is well out of it. And he couldn't do any good here." With that she turned and left the room, closing the door behind her.

I undressed, went into the bathroom, took a shower and dressed in fresh underclothes and a white two-piece nylon dress. I decided I'd better keep my hair in a neat bun while I was at the château. That was the way Gloria and Aunt Veronica had always seen me, and that was the way they would expect to see me.

When I went downstairs, there was no one in sight, and it took a while before I found out how to get to the back terrace. I finally decided the best way would be to go out the front door and walk around the outside of the château. But I found even that was rather complicated. There were formal gardens all around, and a gravel path wound through them. When eventually I came to the back of the château where I could see the terrace, I discovered I was below it and would have to go up a flight of uneven rock steps to reach the flagstone terrace where a round umbrella table was set with fine china and silverware. The umbrella was white on the top, with large splashy roses. It was lined in green and had deep white fringe. The place mats on the white wrought-iron table matched the color of the roses on the umbrella. It looked like a picture in *House & Garden.*

Gloria and Aunt Veronica were sitting in wicker lounge chairs, waiting for me. They each had a cocktail glass in one hand. As I came up the steps, Aunt Veronica said, "Oh, there you are. We've been waiting for you. What will you have to drink? We're having martinis."

"That will be fine." I didn't really want anything, but I didn't want to be a difficult guest.

As if she'd been waiting for me to appear, a maid came through open double French doors with a glass pitcher half full of martinis, a glass and a silver dish of salted peanuts on a silver tray. After serving me, she put the tray on a side table which stood against the wall of the building and went inside again. Aunt Veronica called after her, "You may serve lunch in half an hour, Celeste."

The thought flashed through my mind that, even though the servants were French, everyone spoke to them in English.

Gloria looked better. She and her aunt were still wearing the same things they had had on when I arrived, but Gloria had smoothed her hair.

As I sipped my cocktail I looked out over the countryside. It was beautiful. In the far distance was another hill town. I said, "It's very lovely here. What is that town over there?"

Gloria said, "That's Saint Paul. We can drive over for lunch some day. There is a nice inn there with an outside dining terrace. Some of the stalwart English and American tourists walk over and back. It's about twelve kilometers, I think. But personally, I prefer to ride."

Also in the distance I could see a terraced hill covered with colorful flowers. "Those flowers — what are they?" I asked.

"They call them stock," Aunt Veronica told me. "They make perfume from them. We'll have to take you to *Grasse* where they make the perfume sometime, if things go all right."

I saw Gloria give her a quick glance and wondered why things might not go all right.

Gloria asked me, "How did you like Paul?"

"Paul? Who is he?"

She got up and poured herself another cocktail. Returning to her chair and stretching out her legs in front of her, she said, "The man who drove you up from the station."

I said, "Oh, *Monsieur Thireau.* He seems very nice."

I noticed Aunt Veronica shake her head at her niece, but Gloria pretended not to have seen her, although I knew she had. "He *is* very nice," she said, sipping her cocktail. "I was just too young to realize it when I was married to him."

I almost choked on my own cocktail, spilled some of it on my dress and had to wipe it off. "I didn't know," I said.

Quickly Aunt Veronica observed, "That is over and done with."

Gloria finished her drink. "Is it?" she asked. "I wonder."

Celeste came out with a tray of fruit compotes, and Aunt Veronica got up. "Here's our lunch," she said, as if relieved to be able to change the subject.

Celeste placed a compote at each place, then collected our empty cocktail glasses and went inside, and we took our seats at the table. Aunt Veronica said, "Carol, you sit there so you can see the view."

I sat down on the chair she indicated, and Gloria moved around beside me in a position which gave her part of the view; the part that overlooked the snow-capped mountain. "See that long white villa down there in the valley," she said to me. "The one with the high white wall around it and the mimosa tree in the garden and the olive orchard at the side. Those dusty grayish green trees are olive."

It took me a moment to locate it, but finally I did. "It's very nice," I said when I'd pinpointed it. "Is it nice inside?"

"That's where Paul lives now. I've never been inside. He just bought it recently. I want to go over and see it sometime."

Aunt Veronica cleared her throat, but Gloria paid no attention. She went on, "His father, grandfather and great-great-grandfather used to own this château," she told me. "Paul was born here and grew up here. Then my father offered him so much money for it he let him have it. He didn't want to, but after the second world war his family had," she smiled sadly, "financial difficulties."

Aunt Veronica said, "Isn't it a lovely day? The sky is so blue, and the mountain stands out so clearly."

Gloria pushed away her half eaten fruit compote. "I was always suspicious that Paul married me for my money, but now I am beginning to wonder. Of course I know Mark did. But that doesn't matter. He'll do whatever I say. But Paul is a *man*. *I* had to do whatever *he* said." She snickered as if it were a joke.

Crossly Aunt Veronica said, "Keep quiet, Gloria. You're making a fool of yourself."

Gloria sighed and leaned back in her chair. She seemed to have gone suddenly limp. "You're so right," she told her aunt. "But your tense is wrong. I'm not *making;* I've *made!* Past tense."

Chapter Four

After lunch I returned to my room to unpack.

Just as I was finishing, there was a timid knock on the door, and I called, *"Entrez."* The door opened, and Celeste came in. *"Mademoiselle,* if I could speak with you, *s'il vous plaît?"*

I said, *"Oui, certainement."*

She seemed nervous, and I began to feel apprehensive, of what I didn't know.

"Please forgive me," the woman said. For now that I actually took a good look at her, I could see she was older than I'd thought at lunch time. She was short and slender, with curly black chair and large, very shiny dark brown eyes. I judged her to be about forty. "I feel I should warn you, *Mademoiselle,*" she said, twisting her hands together.

"What is it, Celeste?" My feeling of apprehension increased.

She looked nervously around the room, then looked out into the hall. Coming back, she said, "It is that you must not walk around the château at night. It is not safe."

I watched her face and tried not to show my surprise. "Why is it not safe?" I asked. "There is no one here but *Madame* Preston, *Madame* Meyerhoff, myself and the servants. Is there?"

Her eyes seemed to get larger. "No, *mademoiselle*. At least we don't think so."

"What do you mean — you don't think so?"

She shrugged. "Sometimes strange things happen," she said.

"You mean recently, or all the time?"

"Recently."

"Anything specific?"

She hesitated. "*Oui*. Just last week, one of the maids was found dead — under peculiar circumstances."

"What kind of peculiar circumstances?"

"I'm not allowed to say, *mademoiselle*."

"Why not?"

"I would lose my job."

"But why?"

"I cannot tell you, *mademoiselle*. But it was a great tragedy. Everyone liked Janine."

"Was this Janine a new maid, or had she been here for some time?"

"She had been here since before *Monsieur Paul* —" Realizing she had said something she shouldn't have, she stopped, chewed at her lower lip, then said, "When *Monsieur* Graylock bought the château, he kept what servants were left."

"How many servants are there?" My knees began to feel hollow, and I sat down on a nearby chair.

"There are only four — now," Celeste said. "*Jacques,* me, *Madame Fouchette;* she is the cook and housekeeper. When Janine was alive she was just the cook. And *Philippe,* the gardener. He is very old."

"That's not many for such a big place," I said.

Celeste shrugged. "It is not all in use now," she told me. "Just this wing on this floor and the servants' rooms on the third floor of this wing, and the downstairs. The fourth floor of this wing is closed, and the entire wing on the other side."

"Where was this Janine found?" I asked.

"In the courtyard."

"When?"

"In the morning. *Jacques* found her when he came up from the village. He lives down in the village and comes up at six every morning."

"Had it been this girl's night off? Had she been out for the evening?"

"No, *mademoiselle.* Janine was not young. She was fifty-one. She did not have what you call the rendezvous."

I said, "I see. What was her position here? What did she do?"

"She was the housekeeper. She had run the château for twenty-five years. She knew it when *Monsieur Paul* and his father were here. *Madame Fouchette,* she was always jealous of her. But now she has got what she wanted. She is the housekeeper."

I asked, "Is *Monsieur Paul*'s father alive?"

"No, *mademoiselle.* He did not return from the war."

"And his mother?"

"She died when *Monsieur Paul* was seventeen.

She had an accident in the sea. She was drowned."

"That was how long ago?"

"Ten years."

"That makes *Monsieur Paul* twenty-seven now?"

"*Oui, mademoiselle.*"

"Were you here when Mr. Graylock bought the place?"

"*Oui,* I was here. I have been here fifteen years."

"Then you did not know the older *Monsieur Thireau?*"

"*Oui,* I knew him. Everybody knew him. I am from the town. I knew the people up here in the château before I came to work here."

"And how did you feel about the place being sold out of the family?"

Tears came into Celeste's large dark eyes. "We all felt very unhappy about it," she said.

There didn't seem to be anything more to say but, "Well, *merci,* Celeste. I am glad you told me."

"And you will be careful, *mademoiselle?*" Her hands were clasping and unclasping more nervously than ever now.

"Yes, I will be careful."

"And you will take care of the young *madame?*"

"I will try."

"And do not tell her or *madame,* her aunt, that I told you about Janine. They would not like it."

"Were they here when it happened?"

"*Oui,* they were here. Also *Monsieur* Preston and *Monsieur* Graylock."

I said, "Well, *merci* again, Celeste."

She turned and hurried out of the room and quietly closed the door, and I was left alone.

Chapter Five

When I went down to dinner my first night at the château, I heard voices in the drawing room at the left of the foyer.

A man's voice asked, "Why did you come back here?"

Then a woman's voice, which sounded like Gloria's: "I had no choice. My father planned it that way."

"*Sacré bleu!*" the man said, and I recognized the voice as Paul Thireau's. "Aren't you old enough to run your own life *yet?*"

"Old enough, but not strong enough." There was weariness in Gloria's voice. "You know I haven't been well since —"

"Nonsense!" Paul cried. "You are strong as a horse — if you would not drink so much and take so much medicine."

Gloria didn't answer, and I, halfway across the foyer, stopped, not knowing what to do. I didn't want to intrude, nor did I want to stand there and eavesdrop. But the dinner gong had sounded several minutes ago, so I didn't want to return to my room.

Paul began to speak again. "Why did you marry that *ridiculous* man?"

To hear the man I had been in love with referred to as a "ridiculous man" gave me a strange feeling. Instinctively I wanted to rush into the room and refute the statement. Mark might be a fool, a social climber and overly ambitious — but he wasn't ridiculous.

"He is not a ridiculous man," Gloria said. "He is really a dear." Instantly my heart warmed toward her. At least she had the decency to stand up for her new bridegroom.

"You are not in love with him," Paul stated.

"So?" I could imagine Gloria's shrug of insouciance.

"So! So! So! What kind of an answer is that?" Paul cried angrily. "You are in love with *me!* And you know it! Why do you allow yourself to be pushed around by that arrogant father of yours and that overpowering aunt?"

"Get out!" Gloria cried. Then louder, in almost a scream: "*Get out!* You are insulting!"

"And you are a silly little fool. I don't know why I bother with you!" Paul shouted back. Then, before I could decide which way to go, he strode angrily from the room, dashed down the stairs at the side of the fountain and out the front door, slamming it behind him.

I needn't have worried about his seeing me. He was so angry I don't believe he would have seen me if he'd bumped right into me. I sank down on a sofa to keep from having to face Gloria. I felt she should have a few minutes to compose herself before seeing me. But I knew

Aunt Veronica would be appearing at any moment, so after about five minutes I got up and sauntered into the living room.

Gloria was sitting on the sofa crying, her hands covering her face, her slender shoulders shaking. She was dressed in a pale blue dinner dress with a fuchsia belt and matching pumps.

I went over and, sitting down beside her, put an arm around her shoulders. When she saw it was I, she put her head on my shoulder and sobbed.

I let her cry for several minutes, thinking it would do her good; then I said, "There now, pull yourself together. You don't want your aunt to find you crying."

She sat up, pulled a tissue from the belt of her dress and began to wipe her eyes and blow her nose. When she had herself under control, she asked, "Did you see Paul?"

"I saw him go out. I was just coming down the stairs."

"Then you didn't hear what we said?"

"No." What else could I do but lie?

She leaned back against the sofa. She was very pale, and her hands now lay limp in her lap. "Would you mind sleeping in my room with me tonight?" she asked me. "I have a large king-sized bed that can be separated into twin beds."

"If you want me to," I told her. "But why?"

Tears began to roll down her pale cheeks. "Because I'm afraid," she said in a very low voice. "Afraid," she repeated, like a soft echo.

Before I could ask her what she was afraid of, Aunt Veronica came into the room. She looked extremely handsome in a low cut black dinner gown. Her blue-tinted white hair was upswept, and there were diamonds glittering on her ear lobes.

"Well, I hope you are hungry, Carol," she said, ignoring Gloria and sitting in a high-backed tapestry chair across the room from us. "We are having a typically French dinner in your honor."

I said, "How nice."

Beside me, Gloria sighed.

Jacques came in with a tray of cocktails. They looked like martinis again. Tonight he was dressed as a butler, and his service was perfect. He was a man about forty, rather nondescript. I began to wonder about him.

Our dinner was delicious. It was served in the dining room, which was just alongside the back terrace where we had lunched. Over an ornate stone fireplace hung the portrait of a distinguished-looking man dressed in a suit in the style of a couple of generations ago. There was a resemblance to Paul Thireau, and I presumed it was his grandfather. With Aunt Veronica there, I decided it wouldn't be polite to ask. But, noticing me looking at it, she said, "That is one of the Thireau men. I don't know which one."

"Paul's grandfather," Gloria said.

"I don't know why your father doesn't have it taken down."

Gloria shrugged. "It's atmosphere. And valuable. It could probably be sold to some Paris gallery for a good price."

"If it was my house, I'd at least have it put up in the attic."

Trying to change the subject, I asked, "Do French châteaus have attics?"

"None of us has ever bothered to go up to see," Gloria told me. "At least I haven't." Then, turning to her aunt: "If Father doesn't want to sell that painting of *Grandpère* Thireau, why can't we give it to Paul?"

"Why should we?" Aunt Veronica asked. "He sold the place, furnished. The painting must have been part of the agreement."

"When Paul sold the place, he was too upset to quibble. And we've thrown out most of the old stuff and refurnished the entire place, that is, the part of it that we use."

"Don't try to make excuses for him!" Aunt Veronica had a habit of tilting her nose and tightening one corner of her mouth when she was displeased. She did so now.

"I'm not making excuses for him," Gloria said. "I just think he got a dirty deal."

"You were glad enough to get away from him and go home."

"I was sick. I didn't know what I was doing. And you didn't help any, nagging at me to go home where I belonged."

As if suddenly remembering my presence, Aunt Veronica said, "Well, let's not air our dirty linen before our guest." Then, pushing a small gold and bejeweled box toward Gloria, "Take your pill."

For a moment I thought Gloria was going to refuse; then she seemed to wilt suddenly, and her frail white hand reached for the box. "Why not?" she said. "Another night — another pill."

After dinner we sat in the drawing room for a while, listening to the radio, but as all the programs were in French, I couldn't follow them very well. On a table were several Parisian magazines, and I passed the time leafing through them. Gloria began to look sleepy and put her head back against the chair. In addition to three martinis before dinner, she had had several glasses of wine with her meal. That, together with the pill, was having an effect.

None of us had anything to say. By nine o'clock it seemed to me it must be at least midnight. I stifled a yawn, and Aunt Veronica saw me. "Why don't you girls go up to bed?" she said. "I'll listen to a couple more programs; then I'll go up, too."

Gloria sighed and stood up. "Come on, Carol. Not much fun down here, anyway."

I got up to follow her, saying, "Good night," to Aunt Veronica.

"*Bonne nuit,*" she said. "If there is anything you want, just ring for Celeste. There is a bell pull beside your bed which rings both in the kitchen and up in Celeste's room, if it is after hours."

I said, "Thank you. I'm sure I have everything." I didn't mention the fact that I was sleeping in Gloria's room.

Gloria's room was large and beautiful. It must surely be the master bedroom, yet it was more feminine than masculine. The walls were paneled in pale blue brocade, the ceiling beautifully painted with angels, large and small, floating through fluffy tinted clouds. The floor was highly polished, with silky, light-colored Persian rugs in strategic places. The bed Gloria had mentioned was indeed a king size, with a pale blue satin tufted headboard and a blue silk cover. Taking off the cover, Gloria and I folded it carefully and laid it over the back of a chair. Then together we pulled the bed apart so it made twin beds. When we finished, Gloria said, "Maybe you can use your room for dressing and bathing, then come in here to sleep."

I said, "All right. But won't your aunt think it strange if she looks in on her way to bed and discovers me in here with you?"

"She won't. She never bothers about me when she comes up to bed. Besides, it's none of her business. Just close your door when you come over here, and she'll never know the difference. She has her breakfast in bed, so we will be up, dressed and downstairs before she gets up in the morning."

When I returned to Gloria's room, she was in bed in the one farther from the door, her hands behind her head. "You know," she said, "I'm kind of glad you've come."

"I'm glad you're glad," I said. "Shall I put out the lights?"

"Please. There is a wall switch there beside the door. It takes care of all of them. And close the door."

"Shall I lock it?"

"No key. They didn't believe in keys to bedrooms in the old days, I guess."

I noticed she had opened several full-length windows, the French type that open like doors instead of sliding up and down the way ours at home do. The windows overlooked the lower part of the town and the sea, and I could see the lights on the boats as they bobbed up and down. I closed the door, snapped off the lights and got into bed. The sheets were like satin and the mattress like a cloud. "Good night," I said with a sigh of contentment. With the lights out, the room seemed very black.

"Good night," Gloria said. "I like you."

Surprised, I couldn't think of an immediate answer. Then the best I could do was, "Thank you. I'm glad you do."

"Don't you like me?"

"Why — er — yes, of course."

"No, you don't. I can tell. But then, why should you? I've never been very friendly to you."

"There was no reason you should be."

"Yes, there was. Just common decency. Besides, I needn't have taken your boy friend away."

"You didn't. That is, Mark and I were just friends."

"No, you were more than that. Mark told me. He was in love with you — until he met me. And I wouldn't be surprised if he still is."

"Nonsense! If he was, he wouldn't have married you."

"Yes, he would. He's ambitious. And I have money — scads of it. As a matter of fact, I have more than my father, which just about burns him up."

I said, "Oh?"

"Yes. It belonged to my mother. That's why my father married her." She sighed. "That's what happens when a girl has money. She gets married for it instead of for herself."

"That can't always be true. There must be some really nice men."

"Ever meet one?"

"Well, I thought Mark was one. And I know my father was."

She yawned. "I'm so sleepy," she said, her voice trailing off. "I took a couple more pills."

"Should you take so many?"

"What's the difference?"

"It might make a lot of difference — sometime."

"So what?" Then she asked, "What's it like to be poor? I mean like you, having to work for a living?"

"It's not so bad. You get used to it."

"At least if a man marries you, you know it's because he loves you for yourself alone."

"Yes, I guess so."

"You can have Mark back if you want him."

"Thank you, but I don't want him. Not any more."

"He's good as new," Gloria said with a little giggle.

"Even so, that's over, as far as I am concerned."

Gloria yawned again. "Okay. I just thought I'd ask. Good night."

"Good night."

In a few minutes I heard her rhythmic breathing and could tell she was asleep. Then I relaxed myself and must have fallen asleep almost instantly and slept for quite a while until something disturbed me.

Gradually I became conscious of something touching my arm. I moved it, or rather I tried to move it, but couldn't. Something was holding it, and there was a cold wet spot at the bend of the elbow, on the inside. I could hear breathing; not Gloria's. It was nearer, heavier. I managed to open my eyes. The room was no longer as dark as it had been when I'd gone to bed. Now an almost full moon was shining in the windows, making it bright enough for me to see the large form bending over me. My heart began to pound, and for a split-second I was paralyzed with fear. A man in a white hospital coat was bending over me. He had a square-cut beard, and with one hand he was holding my arm; in the other hand he had a hypodermic needle poised to jab into my arm. Suddenly, gaining strength from my fear, I yanked away from him, jumped out of the other side of the bed and began to scream. The man hurried out of the room and quietly closed the door after him.

I stood there screaming until I realized it wasn't going to get me anywhere. Then I stopped. I ran over to the door, snapped on the light, opened the door and looked out into the hall. There was no one in sight, and Aunt Veronica's door was closed. Or was it just closing — stealthily? I shut our door and looked over at Gloria. She was sleeping soundly. Neither my screaming nor the lights had disturbed her.

I looked at my arm. The wet place had dried. I smelled of it. Alcohol. The man had dabbed alcohol on my vein preparatory to jabbing me with the needle. But why? Who was he? What did he have against me? Or had he thought I was Gloria? I was in the bed near the door, where Gloria would have been if I hadn't been there, and perhaps he hadn't noticed the bed had been separated into two sections.

Suddenly I began to feel weak and shaky. I put a straight-backed chair beneath the doorknob, snapped off the light and got back into bed. It was a long time before I could stop shaking and fall asleep again.

The next time I woke up, the sun was shining and the room was bright and cheerful. I looked over at Gloria. She was still asleep. There was a gilt clock on a white marble fireplace at the end of the room. It was pointing to twenty minutes past eight. I stretched, yawned and felt completely relaxed. This was the life. Then I remembered what had happened in the night. Instantly I was tense. Who could the man be? How could he be there in the château in the middle of the night without someone knowing he was there? Was he the one who had killed Janine? Was he planning on killing me? Or Gloria? And why, when I screamed bloody murder, hadn't someone heard me and come to see what was the matter?

I heard Gloria sigh and turned my head. She was awake now and lay watching me. She looked better than she had the day before. I said, *"Bon jour."* She smiled and said, *"Bon jour* yourself."

I asked, "Did you sleep well?"

"Fine. The best I have since I've been here this time. Usually I have such bad nightmares that I wake up exhausted."

"It looks like a nice day."

She glanced over at the windows. "Yes, it does. Let's go somewhere."

"Where?"

"Oh, any place to get away from here. Over to Saint Paul for lunch. Or down to see Paul." Then she smiled. "That's funny; Saint Paul and

Paul Thireau. I never thought of it before. But of course the town wasn't named after him. But maybe he was named after the town. Or his grandfather was."

"Or both place and people were named after Paul the Apostle in the Bible."

She looked disappointed. "I suppose that's it." She stretched and yawned. "Let's get up," she said, rolled over and got out of bed. I did likewise. As we were putting on our slippers and robes, Gloria said, "Meet you down on the back terrace in half an hour. We'll have breakfast there and then go somewhere before Aunt Veronica gets up and tries to stop us. We won't even come upstairs again before we go."

"Why should your aunt want to stop us?" I asked. "Maybe she would like to come along."

"Why should she want to stop us? Because she doesn't like me to go anywhere unless she is with me. And she doesn't go out much herself when she's here."

I had no answer for that, because I didn't understand any of it, so I just said, "Well, I'll go over to my room and get dressed and see you down on the terrace. And by the way, how do you get out on the terrace without going out the front door and walking around?"

She giggled. "Through the dining room, silly," she said.

I felt foolish. I should have been able to figure that out for myself.

I had a quick shower and dressed in a light knit

suit of avocado green with a white shell blouse. I didn't have too many pairs of shoes with me because shoes take up so much room in a bag and also make it heavy. But I had a pair of bone pumps trimmed with a band of brown which had stacked heels of a medium height which I had found comfortable for walking. I chose those.

I made it a point to get down on the terrace before Gloria, because I wanted to talk to Celeste, if I saw her.

She must have been watching for me, because as soon as I reached the terrace she came out after me. *"Bon jour, mademoiselle,"* she said brightly. *"Vous avez bien dormi?"*

I said, *"Ah oui, merci."* Then I switched to English. "Celeste, I want to talk to you. It's urgent!"

She glanced back into the dining room, then up at the windows of the château that were above the terrace. In a low voice she said, "Not here. Come; I will show you the flowers at the bottom of the garden."

I followed her down the rock steps up which I had come the day before. When we were far enough from the château, she stopped and began to show me some roses. Handling them and acting as if she were telling me about them, she said, "Now, no one can hear us here, unless that Philippe comes along. What is it?"

"A man," I said. "A big man in a white doctor's coat. He had a square-cut beard. I woke up in the night, and he was bending over me. He was just about to jab me with a hypodermic needle."

"*Oh, mon dieu!*" Celeste breathed. "Are you sure?"

"Very sure. But I got away from him and screamed. I almost screamed my head off, but nobody came. And he got away."

"*Oh, mon dieu! Mon dieu!*" She crumpled a very beautiful pink rose she had been fingering, and the petals fell to the ground.

"Do you know who he is?" I asked.

"No, *mademoiselle*. I do not know."

We saw Gloria come out on the terrace, and I asked quickly, "Could he have thought I was Gloria?"

"That I do not know. If he came into your room — ?"

"He didn't. I slept in Gloria's room last night. She asked me to. We separated the beds, and I was in the one near the door."

Gloria was waiting for us. She was sitting at the table and looking over the countryside toward Paul's villa.

Celeste said, "We had better go to her. She will become impatient," and started up the rock steps.

Following her, I asked, "Didn't you hear me screaming last night?"

Over her shoulder she said, "*Oui, mademoiselle*. We all heard you. But we dared not go down to see what was the matter."

"Why not? Because of Janine?"

"*Oui.*"

By then we were within a few steps of the terrace, and Gloria called to us, "*Bon jour,* Celeste. Carol, you toad! You beat me getting dressed." She had on a pastel paisley shift with flat-heeled white shoes. Around her head she had a three-cornered scarf of the same material. She looked very pretty. It was easy to understand how Mark or any other man could fall in love with her for herself alone. But I was sure she would never believe that.

We had a typically French breakfast of hot chocolate, *croissants* and strawberry preserves. Gloria explained, "When I am here, I stick to the French idea of breakfast. But you can have bacon and eggs or ham, if you want, or an omelette."

I said, "No, this is fine. I got used to the French breakfast while I was in Paris."

"We can have an early lunch," Gloria said. "Where shall we go? We could go over to Nice and lunch at the Negresco."

I didn't know what to say. I knew what she really wanted to do was go to see Paul, perhaps to patch up their quarrel of the previous evening. I wondered how Paul would welcome us. Or would he refuse to see us? Or he might not even be at home.

Chapter Six

We had both brought our purses downstairs with us when we went down for breakfast, so we were all ready to leave as soon as we finished eating. Our ultimate decision was to drive over to Saint Paul. Gloria said she had a Citröen garaged down in the town. She could have telephoned to have it brought, but I thought it would do us good to walk down the hill. So off we went, after instructing Celeste to tell Aunt Veronica to expect us when she saw us, that we didn't know where we were going.

Gloria was a good driver, but a fast one, and several times I held my breath as she zoomed around curves that had a deep drop on one side of the road and a hill going up on the other. It was a pretty ride, and after we turned one particularly sharp curve I got my first close view of Saint Paul. It was like a fairyland town, white and shining as the sun shone on it.

"I hope they have had the orphans out for their walk before we reach the village," Gloria said. "If you come along when they are out, there is nothing you can do but stop and wait until they go by. And since I lost my baby, seeing children makes me feel badly."

I turned to see tears running down her white cheeks and her hands gripping the wheel so tightly her knuckles seemed almost to be pushing through the tightened skin. "I'm sorry. I didn't know," I said.

She must have sensed my unspoken question, because she said, "It only lived a few hours. It was premature, and Paul was away. Shortly before, he had sold the château to us and — well, he and I weren't getting along too well, so he left me. No, that isn't true. I sent him away. I told him I never wanted to see him again and that I hoped the baby would die."

Suddenly she was struggling to hold back choking sobs, and the car was wobbling on the road alarmingly. I said, "You'd better let me drive until you're feeling better."

She stopped the car, and we changed seats. As far as I could see, the road was fairly straight from where we were into the town. After I'd driven a few minutes, Gloria said, "And that is why I take pills. I feel as if it was my fault, as if I was a murderer. I'd willed the poor little thing to die." She gulped back a sob. "But I hadn't meant it. I just said it to annoy Paul. He wanted a son so badly, and I really wanted to give him a son. I loved him. But I knew — or thought — he had only married me for my money. And for that I hated him — and his child."

I reached over and gently patted her hands that were clenched in her lap. "Don't blame yourself. You couldn't have killed the baby just by wishing. You know that."

By the time we reached the village, she had quieted down, and I gave a sigh of relief. Then, down at the end of the main street, I saw a group of children coming toward us. They were being led by several nuns with large, starched white wing-like hats and long blue robes. The children were all dressed alike, in black smock-like aprons. The little boys had short pants beneath the aprons. Beside me Gloria cried, "Oh no!"

"Can I turn and go back?" I asked. "Or turn down another street?"

She slouched down in the seat beside me with a groan. "No. We're stuck until they pass. You'll just have to park here at the side."

As the children drew nearer, I could see their faces. They looked happy, well fed, and they were scrupulously clean. They ranged in age from about three to the early teens. One little fellow, the smallest of the lot, was having trouble keeping pace with the bigger children. One of the nuns, looking back, saw his dilemma and said something to a strong-looking girl of about fourteen. The girl went back, picked the child up in her arms and carried him.

When they came closer to us, I felt Gloria give a start. She sat up on her seat, stiff and tense. When the girl carrying the child reached the car, she cried out, *"Attendez! Venez ici, s'il vous plaît."*

The girl came close to the car, and the child smiled and reached a chubby hand to Gloria.

She took it and held it. "How old is he?" she asked the girl in French

"*Troisans,*" the girl told her.

"He is an orphan?"

"*Oui, mademoiselle.* We all are." As they stood there in the bright sunshine, I could see why Gloria was attracted by the child. He looked very much like Paul Thireau: the same color hair, the same gray eyes, the same facial expression.

Gloria asked, "*Quel est votre nom?*"

The child smiled. "Paul," he said.

I felt a quiver go through Gloria. The girl said, "The nuns, they named him after the town. We have quite a few Pauls in the home."

One of the nuns came back to see what was keeping her charges. After exchanging pleasantries with Gloria and giving me a smile and a nod, she said, "He is our pet — this one."

Gloria let go of his hand and smoothed his wavy dark brown hair from his face. "He is very cute," she said. "You do not know who his parents were?"

"No, *mademoiselle.* And if we did, we would not be allowed to tell. We found him in the chapel one morning. That is all we know."

"How old was he when you found him?"

"He was new-born. He could not have been more than a day old."

Gloria leaned back in her seat. I could see she was tense and even paler than usual. "He looks like someone I know," she said.

"Perhaps you would like to visit us sometime?" the nun suggested.

Shrinking back, Gloria said, "Oh, no. No. *Merci.* Forgive me for detaining your charges."

"That is all right. Good day, *mademoiselle.*" The nun turned away, and the girl carrying the child followed her. Over the girl's shoulder the child called, *"Au revoir."*

After they had gone, Gloria and I sat there without talking. The street was clear now the children had passed. I asked, "Shall we go now?"

Gloria nodded. "Yes. They won't be back this way. You'd better let me drive now. I know the way up to the inn."

I didn't think she was in any condition to drive, but maybe it would be good for her to do something besides sit there and think. So we changed seats again. As she took the wheel, I noticed her hands were trembling, but she drove carefully enough, and it wasn't far to the inn. There was a parking space at the side, and we left the car with the attendant and went into the building. We walked through a large, cool dining room and out onto a good-sized flagged terrace that overlooked the surrounding country. We were too far away to have a view of the sea, but there was an entrancing view of well kept farms and terraced gardens.

Bright umbrellas shaded the tables, and we chose a table beside a hedge that fenced off the terrace from the ground that descended from it. It was too early for lunch, but at a couple of tables were women, definitely tourists, having a late breakfast.

When a waitress came to us, Gloria asked for, *"De l'eau, s'il vous plaît."* To me she said, "I need a pill after that."

"Not a sleeping pill?" In spite of the sun on my back, I felt a chill.

"No. A tranquillizer. Don't worry. It's perfectly safe. My father gets them for me from one of his clients."

The waitress brought a carafe of water and glasses and poured us each a glass. Gloria opened her purse and took out a small cloisonné box. In it were several long oval pills. She put one in her mouth and sipped some water.

The waitress stood waiting for our order, and Gloria said, "May we sit here for a while? It's a little early for lunch." She looked at a wrist watch she was wearing. It was a quarter to eleven.

The waitress said, *"Oui, mademoiselle,"* and left us.

After she'd gone, Gloria sighed. "I wish we hadn't seen that child," she said. "It was upsetting."

"Is that the first time you've seen him?"

"Yes. This is the first I've been away from the château since we came down two weeks ago. And — well, I haven't been in France in three years."

We both gazed out at the view for several minutes without talking. As far as I was concerned, I couldn't think of anything to say.

Then, without looking at me, Gloria said, "If my baby had lived, I would have wanted him to look just like that."

"Perhaps he would have had light hair, like you."

"No."

"Did you see him before — ?"

She shook her head, and tears began to run down her pale cheeks. "No. They thought it best I shouldn't."

"Who were *they?*"

"Aunt Veronica and the doctor."

"Then you don't know whether he had dark or light hair? Boys are supposed to look like their mothers and girls like their fathers." Then the thought struck me that Gloria didn't look anything like her father.

"The Thireau boys always are the image of their fathers." She fumbled in her purse for a package of tissues, found one and wiped her eyes. Then she looked at me, and her eyes were wide with anger. "If I thought he — I couldn't bear it!"

She clenched her hands and pounded the table until the umbrella above us wobbled and the glasses and the carafe teetered. I caught the carafe before it went over. "What do you mean?" I asked, wishing Aunt Veronica were there to handle the situation.

Gloria glared at me. Her jaw was tense, her lips tight over her small even white teeth, and her breathing was rapid. The tranquillizer hadn't had time to take effect. "I mean if I thought for a minute Paul had had an affair with another girl and that child was the result, I'd kill him!"

Her voice rose to a high pitch, and the late breakfasters looked at us. I said, "Ssshhh!"

"I don't care. I would!"

"No, you wouldn't. Besides, if what you are imagining really had happened, he wouldn't have allowed the child to be placed in an orphanage."

"He might not have known about the child. Why, there may be others — in other orphanages!" She was trembling now, almost on the verge of hysteria. I was beginning to be frightened. What could I do to calm her?

I got up and pulled my chair around, sat down beside her and put an arm around her shaking shoulders. "Come now," I said. "Take it easy. You're letting your imagination run away with you. I don't know Paul very well, but I don't believe he is the kind of a man who would go dashing around the country having illegitimate children like a rabbit."

The simile struck her as funny, and she giggled. Then I could feel her relaxing. The pill, I hoped, was beginning to take effect. She sighed and leaned back in her chair. "No," she said. "Paul isn't like that. As a matter of fact, he is very strait-laced."

I patted her shoulder. "Well, then, stop being silly." I got up and pulled back my chair to where

I'd been before. "Why don't we have lunch now?" I suggested. "All this fresh air is making me hungry."

She motioned to our waitress, who was hovering at one side. Before she reached us, Gloria asked me, "Martini?"

I said, "No thanks. And if you have one, I am going to drive home."

She shrugged. "You don't want anything?"

"I'll have a cinzano. It's harmless."

Needless to say, Gloria had two martinis to my one cinzano. The terrace began to fill up with other people, mostly women and mostly English and American, with a few Germans. The buzz of conversation made it easier for us not to talk, and I was relieved to see that Gloria had calmed down.

We had a delicious cheese omelette for lunch, with fresh, crusty French bread and a crisp green salad with a dressing that had a nutty flavor. And of course the inevitable wine of the region. It was very nice, but knowing I was going to do the driving back, I had only about half a glass.

We were nearly to the village of *Fleur-sur-Mer* when Gloria said, "Go on through the main street here, and I'll tell you where to turn off."

"But don't you want to leave the car at the garage?"

"Later. First I want to visit Paul."

I braked so suddenly a car in back of me honked a warning. "But do you think that is a good idea?" I couldn't help asking.

"Good or not, I've got to see him."

"You aren't going to — ?"

"To tell him about that child? I certainly am."

I was driving slowly now, reluctant to do her bidding. "But you can't do that!" I protested. "You can't just go to him and accuse him of —"

"I'm at least going to let him know he can't get away with anything."

We'd reached the end of the village street by then, and off to the left was a dirt road. "Turn here," Gloria directed.

So I turned. What else could I do? I had no authority over her.

We had to make a couple more turns before we came to Paul's place. In the white wall there was a large double iron gate which was wide open. Gloria said, "Drive in and stop over there near the garage. I've never been here before, but he must be home. His cars are here." And they were — the white Mercedes-Benz and a blue station wagon.

He must have heard or seen us, because he came out of a side door. He was wearing gray slacks, a bright blue blazer with brass buttons and a dark red paisley scarf at his throat. *"Bon jour,"* he greeted us, coming over to the car. "Won't you come in?"

Gloria got out of the car and slammed the door. "Shall I wait here for you?" I asked her.

"Of course not. Come on."

Paul opened the door beside me and helped

me out of the car. "It is nice in the garden," he said, leading the way to the back of the house, where I could see a lovely garden and a flagstone terrace upon which were garden chairs and the usual umbrella table. This umbrella was sky blue on top with a lining and fringe of cream. It was shady and cool on the terrace, and I was glad to relax in a comfortable chair.

Gloria wandered around the garden, inspecting the flowers, and Paul stood and watched her. Slowly she sauntered back to the terrace. When she reached Paul, she smiled up at him. "You look very nice," she said. "New jacket?"

He said, "No. Won't you sit down? I'll get some cold drinks."

Gloria sat gracefully in an arm chair. "Gin and tonic for me," she said sweetly.

"Iced tea for all of us," Paul said, and went into the house.

Watching him go, Gloria raised her eyebrows and smiled slightly. "He really is handsome," she said.

"Yes, he is," I agreed.

He returned in a moment and sat down between us. "Marie will bring it out in a few minutes," he said. Then he asked, "Aunt Veronica did not come with you?"

"We ran away right after breakfast, before she was up," Gloria explained.

"You have lunched out?"

"Yes. Over at Saint Paul." As she spoke, Gloria watched his face.

He asked, "At the inn? They have very good food there. Or they used to have. I haven't been over in several years."

I said, "Yes. It was delicious. And it is a very pretty place."

Interrupting me, Gloria said, "On the way over we met the orphans out for their walk."

"Poor little devils," Paul said compassionately.

"Yes, quite." Gloria kept watching him. "There is a little three-year-old boy who is the image of you."

He gave her a surprised look, then smiled. "How interesting," he said.

"Yes, isn't it?" Gloria agreed. "Do you remember that picture of you when you were three? You showed it to me just after we were married."

He said, "Yes. I have it in my desk."

"Could we see it?"

He looked annoyed, but he stood up. "Why, I suppose so," he said, and went into the house. While he was inside, a middle-aged maid brought us tall glasses of iced tea with a sprig of mint in each glass. There was also a plate of little cakes. The maid returned to the house, and Paul came out. He had a snapshot in his hand. Giving it to Gloria, he said, "Here it is."

She took it and studied it carefully for a moment. Then she leaned over and gave it to me without a word, but with a look of triumph in her eyes. In my turn I examined the picture. It could have been of the child we'd seen over in Saint Paul, only this child was dressed in an expensive-looking suit. I looked up at Paul. I didn't know what to say.

He took his glass of iced tea from the table and passed the plate of cakes. Then he sat down. After a moment he said, "Could you tell me what this is all about?"

Gloria sipped her tea. "Just this: That child over in Saint Paul looks exactly like that picture of you when you were three."

"So?"

"The Thireau men always look like their fathers."

Paul almost choked on his tea. *"Sacré bleu!"* he exploded. "Are you accusing me of — of — !" He couldn't finish.

"I am not accusing you of anything," Gloria said. "I just think it is strange."

He stared at her. "Are you trying to say that you think — ?"

"I just think you are a man. And men, particularly Frenchmen, do not think anything of having affairs."

He gave her a long, steady look before saying, "Has it occurred to you that I have not had a wife for three years, so that I am free to do whatever I wish?"

Tears sprang to her eyes, and she didn't answer. I wanted to get up and run, but I couldn't very well without making things worse, and for several minutes we all sat so still

I could hear the birds twittering in the garden and in the mimosa tree at the side. Paul put his glass of tea on the table and took a cigarette case from a pocket, passed it to me and, when I shook my head, lit one for himself. When he had it going, he said quietly, "You surprise me, Gloria. I never would have believed it would make any difference to you if I took a mistress."

She chewed at her lips to hold back the sobs and didn't answer him. He waited for a moment, then said, "If it will make you feel better, I swear to you that I have never had but one child, our child. It is a mere coincidence that the child over in Saint Paul resembles me. I am very sorry for him, and I shall do what I can for him, even though he is not mine."

Gloria put her glass on the table, got up and ran to the car, got in and slammed the door. There was nothing for me to do but follow her. Walking beside, Paul asked, "Does the child really resemble me?"

I looked up at his handsome face. It was very serious. "Yes, it does," I told him. "It is the image of you."

He shook his head as if he couldn't believe it. "Strange," he said. Then, "I swear to you, *mademoiselle,* the child couldn't possibly be mine. Since I lost my wife, I have lived a life of celibacy."

"I believe you," I told him.

As he helped me into the car, he whispered in

my ear, "Take care of her."

I nodded and backed the car around so I could go out the gates. As I drove back to the village, I could hear Gloria sniffling beside me.

Chapter Seven

When we returned to the château, Aunt Veronica was waiting for us. She was in a state, pacing back and forth in the drawing room. As soon as we entered the hallway, she rushed toward us. "Where have you been?" she demanded angrily.

"Out." Gloria pushed past her, went into the drawing room and sank down on the sofa. We had left the car at the garage in the village and walked up the hill.

Aunt Veronica went and stood in front of her. "Where have you been?" she demanded again.

Gloria sighed. "I told you. Out. After all, I'm a grown woman. I don't have to account to you for every move I make." She closed her eyes and leaned her head back.

Aunt Veronica's black eyes flashed angrily. "You do as long as we are here and I am responsible for you."

Gloria opened her eyes and rolled them upward. "Oh, go away!" she said, and closed her eyes again.

Aunt Veronica turned to where I had sat down in the high-backed tapestry chair near the doorway. "Carol, *you* tell me. Where have you been all day?"

I didn't know what to say. My sympathies were more and more with Gloria, and I didn't want to tattle. When I didn't answer, Gloria opened her eyes again. "Don't badger Carol. I'll tell you. We had lunch at the inn over in Saint Paul, and then we drove back and over to Paul's, and he gave us some iced tea." I waited for her to mention the child we had seen in Saint Paul, but she didn't. And for some reason I was glad.

Pacified for the moment, Aunt Veronica turned and marched from the room. She didn't even look at me as she passed me, and I had the feeling I was in the doghouse.

After she'd gone, Gloria said, "Thanks, pal."

"What for?"

She opened her eyes and looked at me. "For keeping your mouth shut."

"You aren't going to tell her about — ?"

"No. And please don't you."

"I won't."

She got up from the couch. "I think I'll go up and take a nap before dinner." She looked at her wrist watch. "It's four o'clock. See you later."

I said, "Okay. Is it all right if I go out and sit on the back terrace for a while?"

"Sure. Why not? Go wherever you please, any time."

"Thank you."

"Except that I think Aunt Veronica has gone

out there, and if she sees you she'll try to pump you."

I said, "Oh. Well, then I'd better go up to my room."

So we went up to the second floor together. Gloria went into her room, said, "See you," and closed the door, and I went on down the hall toward my room. As I passed Aunt Veronica's room, I noticed the door was open, for the first time since I'd arrived, but she wasn't there. Curious, I stopped in the doorway and glanced around. It was a lovely room, similar to mine, with French provincial furniture and hangings, bedspread and rug of apple green. I started to turn away when a large silver-framed picture on the dresser caught my eye. I stepped into the room and walked over to get a better look at it. It was a portrait photograph of a very handsome middle-aged man with graying light hair and a square-cut beard.

I turned to leave the room and saw Aunt Veronica standing in the doorway watching me. She asked, "You want something?"

I'd never been so embarrassed in my life. I knew my face must have instantly flushed a flaming red. I said, "No. I was just admiring your room."

She came into the room. "And my husband's picture?"

"I — er — is that your husband?" I stammered.

She went over to the dresser and picked up the

picture, holding it in both hands and gazing down at it. "He was," she said. "He is dead now."

"I'm sorry." I began walking to the doorway, anxious to get away.

Behind me she said, "So am I. I loved him very much."

At the door I turned. "Forgive me for entering your room," I said. "It is so pretty I couldn't help admiring it."

She put the photograph into a dresser drawer and closed the drawer with a bang. "That's all right," she said. "We'll have cocktails in the drawing room at six-thirty."

Glad to get away, I said, "Okay. See you later."

As I went on down the hall to my own room, I heard her door close.

I had expected Aunt Veronica to be unpleasant when we met for dinner, but she wasn't. To my surprise, and I think Gloria's as well, she was charming. She spoke of many things, none of them touching on anything personal to any of us.

Our evening was a repetition of the previous one, and when Gloria and I said good night to her and went up to bed, I went into Gloria's room with her, asking, "Do you want me to sleep in here with you tonight?"

She said, "No, thanks. I'll be all right tonight. Today has done me good. Just having you around is better medicine than all my pills." There was a heavy glass paperweight on a table, and she picked it up and examined it. It was the kind with a tiny scene inside. She shook it, and the scene was covered with snow. I'd seen similar ones before, but this was an unusually large one.

"I'm glad you enjoyed our day," I said. But I couldn't help wondering if seeing Paul and having him tell her of his faithfulness wasn't the real reason, rather than my company. At the door, I hesitated. How could I get her to barricade her door against the man with the square-cut beard without upsetting her? And if I told her about him and she knew who he was, would she believe me? If he was her uncle, who she thought dead, what would it do to her?

I decided there was nothing I could do without frightening her, so I said, "Well, good night. Shall I meet you on the back terrace for breakfast?"

She said, "Yes. About the same time. If it is a nice day, we can go over to Nice for lunch. There are some attractive shops on the *Avenue Victor Hugo*. Even if you don't want to buy anything, it is fun to window-shop."

When I reached my room, I closed the door, then looked around for something to prop beneath the knob. There wasn't an appropriate straight-backed chair that was strong enough. The best I could do was to pull the *chaise longue* over in front of it. At least it would hamper anyone trying to get into the room, and if the door hit against it as it was being opened, it would probably awaken me.

After I'd undressed, bathed and was ready for bed, I stepped out onto the stone balcony outside my windows. It was a beautiful night; the stars hung low in the dark velvet sky. The moon had not yet risen. I could hear the water trickling in the fountain in the *Place* and see the lights down in the town, and beyond, the lights on the boats on the water. I leaned out and tried to see down the road to the village, but it was too dark. And few of the houses showed lights. The people who lived in those houses got up early in the morning and went to bed early at night. I looked up to see if there were any lights in any of the château windows. There were a couple on the floor above me, probably in the rooms belonging to the servants. Then I saw, or thought I saw, a light in a window on the top floor of the unused portion of the château. But if there had been one, it was quickly extinguished, or curtains were quickly drawn to cover it.

I shivered and went inside, put out my own lights and got into bed. A loud buzzing mosquito kept me awake for a while but finally went away, and eventually I fell asleep. Some time later I was awakened by a slight noise. Immediately fear gripped me. I lay still, listening, my flesh cold, my heart racing. I watched the door. Was it moving? Was the handle turning? I sat up, holding my breath, my eyes straining to see through the darkness of the room. The *chaise longue* was still in place, but slowly, menacingly, it was moving as the door was pushed against it. I jumped out of bed, cried, "Who is there?" and stumbled toward the door, kneeling on the *chaise longue* and, with all my strength, pushing the door closed. At first there was opposition; then suddenly there was none, and the door closed with a sharp click. Whoever had been pushing it had stopped. I knelt there, leaning my whole weight against the closed door. "Go away!" I cried as loudly as I could. "And stay away from Gloria!"

I knelt there for a long time, pushing against the door and listening for a sound in the hall. But there was nothing, and I was too frightened to move my barricade and look out into the hall. Whomever it was who walked the halls at night, carrying a hypodermic needle, I was sure he was no ghost. And I knew I would stand little or no chance against him if I encountered him. And if I did meet him and screamed for help, no one would come to my aid. That had been proven last night.

After a long time, I decided I had frightened him away by calling out and pushing the door closed. But I didn't feel safe going back to bed, so I brought a pillow and a blanket over and finished the night on the *chaise longue*. That way, if the door was again opened and the *chaise longue* moved, I would be instantly aware of it. And with my added weight on the *chaise longue,* it wouldn't move so easily.

In the morning I was awakened by the changing of the church bell in the *Place*. It wasn't Sunday, so it must be a saint's day. The noise was deafening. I decided I might as well get up, though it was only six-thirty. I took a leisurely bath, then lay down again for a while. By that time the bell had stopped clanging. When I was dressed and ventured out of my room, Gloria's door was still closed, as was Aunt Veronica's. So I went down to the back terrace to wait for Gloria in the early morning sunshine. It was another beautiful day; the gardens looked dewy fresh, and the scent from the flowers was sweet and pleasant.

In a moment Celeste came out. *"Bon jour, mademoiselle,"* she said. And as she had the morning before, she asked if I had slept well.

I shook my head, and her face paled. In a whisper she asked, "The same reason?"

Keeping my own voice low, I said, "I think so."

"You did not see?"

"No. I was in my own room, and I had the door barricaded with the *chaise longue*. In the middle of the night someone tried to get in." As I talked, Celeste had been moving things around on the tables as if she were serving breakfast. "Miss Gloria?" she asked *sotto voce*.

Philippe, the gardener, an elderly man with stooped shoulders, was working in the garden. He kept watching me out of the corner of his eye, and I thought he had an ugly look.

I said, "I don't know. Her door is closed. Perhaps I should go up and see."

"I will go. But first I will bring you your breakfast." She went into the house and in a few minutes came out with my breakfast. As I drank the chocolate and nibbled at the hot *brioche,* I looked out across the countryside to where Paul's villa snuggled in the valley. I wondered if I should confide in Paul. Would he know who the man with the square-cut beard was? Could he do anything about it if he did? Should the police be called in? I wished the old gardener would go somewhere else. There was something about him that made me feel uneasy.

Celeste returned, looking frightened and upset. "*Mademoiselle* Gloria is awake," she told me. Then she lowered her voice so *Philippe* wouldn't hear her. "But she is in one of her depressions," she added.

"Should I go to her?" I dropped my piece of *brioche* on my plate.

Celeste shook her head. "It would be no use," she said. "When she is like that, it just has to wear off."

"But can't her aunt do something? At least send for a doctor?"

Celeste's shoulders sagged. "No, *mademoiselle,* it is no use. *Madame* Meyerhoff is not sympathetic to her niece. More chocolate?" she asked me as *Philippe* came closer to the terrace to rake around some rosebushes.

I said, "No, thank you." I left the table and went into the house and upstairs. At Gloria's door, I listened a moment. There was no movement inside, so I opened the door and went in. The beds had been left separated, and Gloria was in the one near the door, where I had slept the night before last. Her eyes were closed. I walked over to the bed and said softly, "Gloria."

She opened her eyes and looked up at me, but I was sure she didn't see me. There was a glazed, vacant look in her eyes, and she was as limp as a rag doll. Her arms were lying on the outside of the pale blue sheet covering her. I leaned over and looked at the arm nearest me, at the inside of the elbow. The skin over the vein had an infinitesimal red dot, as if it had been pricked by a hypodermic needle.

For a moment I was too horrified to move. When I could, I went to my room, changed to the shoes I'd worn yesterday, took my purse and hurried downstairs. I didn't see anyone around, and as far as I knew no one saw me. I hurried out of the château and through the arch into the *Place*. It was empty, and I crossed it and began walking down the hill to the village. It was going to be a long walk to Paul's place, but I had to make it.

Before I reached the end of the village, it began to warm up, and I still had several miles to go. I hoped Paul would be at home and that he would offer to drive me back. The church bell was ringing again, and I couldn't help noticing how far the sound carried.

It was nearing eleven when I turned into the gates at Paul's. Both his cars were in the garage, and I thought, Thank goodness.

There was no one in sight, so I had to go to the front door and twist the handle that would ring the bell on the inside of the door. In a moment the door opened, and Marie asked, *"Que désirez-vous, mademoiselle?"*

Not knowing whether or not she spoke English, I said, *"Monsieur Thireau, s'il vous plaît."*

As I talked she had been examining my face, and I could see she remembered me from yesterday. *"Entre?"* she said, led me into a beautifully furnished living room and left me.

I could hear voices somewhere at the back of the house, and in a couple of minutes I heard manly footsteps approaching and Paul came into the room. I thought he looked surprised and somewhat disturbed at seeing me, but he smiled politely. *"Mademoiselle,"* he said. Then, "Is Gloria not with you?"

I said, "No. But it is about her I have come. I am worried about her, frightened for her. There is something strange going on up at the château."

He sat down near me and lit a cigarette. Today he had on gray slacks and a navy turtle-necked sweater. When he'd finished lighting his cigarette, he looked at me, and a kindly expression came into his gray eyes. "You are overheated. Did you walk?"

I nodded. "Yes. It's getting kind of warm."

He got up, went into the hall and called, "Marie!"

From a distance Marie called, *"Oui, monsieur?"*

"Café glacé pour mademoiselle." He turned to me. "Marie will bring you a glass of iced coffee. I hope you like it?"

"It sounds wonderful."

He sat down in a chair nearer to me. "Now what is wrong?"

I didn't stop to analyze whether I could or could not trust this man. Something within me told me I could. And at this point I had nothing to go on but my woman's intuition. So I told him everything I knew and what had happened since the time he had met me at the station, leaving out, of course, the conversations between Gloria and her aunt about him.

He listened intently, leaning over with his elbows on his knees and watching his cigarette burn without smoking it. When I finished, he looked up at me. "It is a delicate situation," he said. "I have no right to interfere. I no longer have any claim on Gloria. And the family does not make me welcome at the château."

"But the police — couldn't you go to them?"

"On what grounds? Gloria has not been harmed. Nor have you."

"What about the girl who was murdered, Janine?"

He gave a start of surprise. "You have heard about that?"

"Yes."

"Who told you?"

"I promised not to say."

"Not Gloria or her aunt?"

"No."

A frown of annoyance furrowed his brow. He thought for a moment, then said, "Since you were here yesterday, I have been doing a lot of thinking."

"About the child?"

"*Oui*. It is strange. Tell me more about it."

So I told him just what had happened, what the nun had said and how the child looked.

He got up and began pacing back and forth the length of the room. "Then the child was found in the chapel just about the time our child died? That was June 2nd, 1964." He darkened his cigarette in an ash tray on a table and resumed his pacing, now with his hands rammed into the pockets of his slacks, his head bowed.

I said, "Yes, it would seem that way."

"And I was away. Anything could have happened."

I gasped. "You don't think — ?"

He stopped in front of me and looked down at my upturned face. "I don't know what to think," he said, his jaw tightened, his teeth clenched. "They are a strange lot."

"Oh, but you can't mean Mr. Graylock," I cried. "Why, I was his private secretary for three years, and he was always very nice."

"Nice he may be, when it suits his purpose. But he is a dangerous man to cross."

"Did you cross him?"

"You could call it that. I demanded he let go of his daughter after I had married her."

"And he wouldn't?"

He shook his head. "He not only wouldn't, but he kept nagging her about me, telling her I was one of the impoverished noblemen of France and had only married her for her money. He either stayed here with us himself or had Aunt Veronica stay with us. We were never left alone except in our bedroom."

I began to feel short of breath. I gripped the arms of my chair with hands that felt cold and trembling. "But I don't understand. How could he do that?"

He sank down on the chair near me again, leaned his elbows on his knees and clasped and unclasped his hands in a tense, nervous manner.

Marie came in with a tall glass of iced coffee with a dab of whipped cream floating on top. She gave it to me on a saucer with a long-handled spoon and a dainty napkin. I said, *"Merci beaucoup,"* and smiled at her.

After she'd left the room, Paul said, "I think I'll ride over to the orphanage and have a look at the child."

I sipped my coffee, which was delicious, with just a touch of cinnamon. "But what shall I do about Gloria? She shouldn't be left at the mercy of whoever that man is."

He leaned back in his chair and lit another cigarette. "You say Aunt Veronica has a photograph of him on her dresser?"

"I am sure it is the same man."

"But she claims he is dead."

"Yes."

He sighed. "I don't think Gloria ever saw her uncle. As the story goes, he was a Nazi who escaped to Italy toward the end of the war and was killed. He had been a doctor before the war. Aunt Veronica met him when she was studying music in Germany, before the Second World War."

"I didn't know she was musical."

"She was a singer, studying for the opera. She has a good voice. I have heard her sing."

I finished the coffee, and Paul jumped up and took the empty glass and saucer from me, placing them on a table. "Would you ride over to Saint Paul with me?"

"Now?"

"Yes."

"If you wish me to."

"I would be glad of your company."

"What are you going to say to the nuns?"

He shrugged. "I'll think of something. Excuse me while I get a coat."

While he was gone, I looked around the room. It was furnished in Swedish modern, with rough, tweedy drapes and a soft beige rug on the floor. A large modernistic painting in colors of the sea, blues and greens, hung over the marble fireplace.

Paul returned, wearing the blue blazer he had

worn yesterday afternoon. I was standing before the fireplace looking up at the painting. "You like my painting?" he asked.

"You mean you did it?"

He smiled. "Guilty."

So he was an artist. I said, "I like it very much. I don't always understand modern art, but this I like. The colors remind me of the sea."

He smiled. "That is what I tried to convey," he said. "Shall we go?"

During the drive to Saint Paul, we talked of art, and for the first time since I'd arrived on the Riviera I relaxed. The sun was warm, even hot, but not unpleasant, and the movement of the car stirred enough breeze to keep us comfortable.

Then suddenly, without warning, a car whizzed past us and cut us off on a sharp curve, and Paul was forced to crash into the hill that rose at our right. I turned my head just in time to catch a glimpse of the driver of the car. It looked like Aunt Veronica. She was wearing her gray dress, and she was driving Gloria's Citroën, which was blue.

"*Sacré bleu!*" Paul cried, and jammed his foot on the brake, throwing me against the windshield. Then he shut off the motor. "Did you see who was in that car?" he asked angrily.

"Yes. It looked like Aunt Veronica."

"Are you sure?"

"Reasonably."

"If it was she, she did it deliberately!" Then he

turned to me. "Are you hurt?" he asked anxiously.

I said, "No, except that I'll probably have a black and blue bump on my forehead from the windshield. But that's my own fault, I didn't have my seat belt fastened. Are you all right?"

"Physically, yes. Mentally, I could commit murder! Which is what she was trying to do."

"Oh no!" I cried. "She wouldn't do that!"

"Don't be too sure. She must have followed you. And she does not want me to go to the orphanage."

"How would she know we were going there?"

"Why else would we be going to Saint Paul?"

"You might be — well, taking me to lunch."

"No, my dear. You would not have run away and walked way over to my place for that."

"But why should she care where we are going, even if she thought we were going to the orphanage?"

He took a pack of cigarettes from his pocket and lit one with the dashboard lighter. His hands were shaking. "I don't know. But I am going to try to find out. She is an excellent driver, and she knows these roads well. That was no accident."

I leaned out of my window and tried to see if there was much damage to the car. As far as I could see, the front and the light were crushed. "Aren't you going to get out and see what the damage to your car is?"

"In a moment." He sat smoking until the cigarette was nearly finished, and I sat beside him, not talking. When he had scrunched out the remaining part of the cigarette in the dashboard ash receptacle, he turned to me, smiled, patted my knee and said, "You are a nice girl. You know when to keep still."

I laughed. "What do we do now? Suppose the car won't start?"

"Then we will walk." He turned the key in the ignition and put his foot on the starter. The motor turned over reluctantly a couple of times and stopped. He uttered something in French which must have been a swear word I didn't know, got out of the car, walked around to the front and examined the damage. Coming back, he said, "I'll have to have it towed. Think you can walk the rest of the way?"

I said, "Sure," and slid over beneath the wheel. He helped me out. There wasn't enough space for me to get out from my side. The car was too close to the side of the hill, and the door wouldn't open.

As we walked along, Paul holding my arm, I said, "What if we meet Aunt Veronica in town?"

"I doubt that we will. She is too smart for that. I am quite sure that she will keep out of our way. There is a back road that will take her around to *Fleur-sur-Mer*. She will probably use that."

"She might have killed us."

"She might have. And herself, too. She was on the outside of the curve. A car dropping from there would have quite a fall, and the passenger would not survive."

I shivered, and he put an arm around me. "It makes me believe the lady is desperate, to take such a chance."

"But why?"

"*That* we will try to find out. At least *I* shall. I would advise you to leave the château at once, today, as soon as you can get back and pack your bags. I'll even come with you and wait, then take you into Nice."

"But what reason could I give for doing that?"

"Say you are ill and must return to Paris. Say anything. But get away. You are not safe there." He was holding me close to his side as if to protect me, and even though he was stirring fear in me, he was also stirring my emotions in a way that was even more frightening to me than the danger that awaited high on the hill at *Fleur-sur-Mer*.

Chapter Eight

When we reached the orphanage, the children were having lunch. The nun who let us in took us to a small, austere sitting room and told us we could wait. Paul explained in French about how I and a friend had met the children the day before and had become interested in the small boy by the name of Paul.

We waited in the cold, cheerless room without talking, but I could tell Paul was nervous. Several times he got up and went to a window, looked out at the lawn for a few minutes, then returned to his chair. Once he said, "I suppose I can't smoke in here."

I said, "I don't believe so. But I am not a Catholic, so I wouldn't know the rules."

To my surprise, he said, "Neither am I. I'm Anglican. One of my grandmothers was English."

After what seemed like an eternity, the nun who had talked to Gloria the day before came in, leading little Paul by the hand. When he saw me, he remembered me, and a bright smile lit up his face. The nun let go of his hand, and he ran to me and cried, *"Ma'm'selle!"* I put my arms around him and gave him a hug; then I turned him toward Paul. "*Monsieur* has come to see you, too," I told him, and my heart skipped like a crazy thing when I saw the child and the man together. They were so alike: the gray eyes, the dark wavy hair, the coloring, the way their hair grew where it met the high forehead, the shape of the ears. It was uncanny.

The child hadn't understood what I'd said to him, but the *monsieur* was enough, and he went to Paul. *"Bon jour, m'sieur,"* he said politely.

Paul took him on his lap, and I saw tears in his eyes. He said in French, "Do you know what my name is?"

The child shook his head.

"Paul."

The child smiled. "Like me," he said.

Paul said, "Yes."

The nun who had brought the child in was sitting quietly in a chair near us. She was looking first at the child, then at the man. I could see the question in her eyes.

Paul talked to the child for a few minutes, all the while examining the little boy's face, his hair, his ears, his hands. Suddenly he turned to the nun. "You do not know who the child's parents were or are?"

"No, *monsieur*."

"You told the ladies yesterday that you found him in the chapel one day."

"That is right, *monsieur*."

"There was nothing on him to identify him?"

"No, *monsieur*. The clothes he was wearing were expensive, but there were no identifying marks on them."

"Have you kept the clothes?"

"*Oui, monsieur.*"

"Could I see them?"

The nun hesitated. "I would have to ask Mother Jennifer," she said. "And it would take time to get them. They are wrapped up and kept in a storeroom."

Paul was hugging the child close to him. "And the date you found him?" he said. "That is important, *very* important."

The nun was watching him with a puzzled look on her placid, kindly face. She said, "The child looks very much like you, *monsieur*."

Paul nodded. Beads of perspiration were standing out on his forehead. "He does," he agreed.

"May I ask, *monsieur*, if you have a child?"

His jaw tightened. "Once I had a son. He did not live."

The nun said, "I am sorry."

"*Merci.* How long would it take to get the clothing?"

"I will ask Mother Jennifer." She got up and left us, and I asked Paul, "Would you recognize the clothing if it had belonged to your son?"

"No. But Gloria should."

I gasped. "But would you dare confront her with it?"

"If there is the slightest chance that the thing

that I am beginning to suspect was done, I would confront the devil with it!"

"But why? Why would they do a thing like that?"

The child was going to sleep in Paul's lap, and Paul rested his cheek against the boy's soft hair. "Money!" he said. "What else?"

"But they have enough money."

"Some people never have enough money," he said bitterly. "And Gloria is a very rich girl. If she had a child, the money would go to the child — if anything happened to her. So there must be no child."

I couldn't speak for a moment. The idea was too horrible. After a few minutes the nun returned with another nun, an older woman wearing steel-rimmed glasses.

Paul stood up to greet her, holding the sleepy child in his arms, and for several minutes they spoke together in French. I could not understand much because they spoke so rapidly. But I could tell Paul was explaining why he wanted the clothing. Mother Jennifer looked serious. Then the younger nun took little Paul, saying, "It is time for his nap."

Paul introduced Mother Jennifer to me, but we could not converse, because the Mother did not speak English and my French wasn't good enough. Paul said something to her, and she nodded. Then Paul and I left.

When we were outside, I asked, "Did you tell her the whole story? I mean, did you tell her what you suspect — that is, that you believe the child to be yours?"

Grimly he said, "Yes. And I warned her to watch him very carefully and not to let any other visitor see him, and until there is some proof I am wrong, not to let him go walking in the town with the others."

"What about the clothing?"

"She will have it for me tomorrow."

"Then you will come back tomorrow?"

"I will."

"What about Gloria?"

"We will go to Gloria now. I will have someone drive us over. And I must arrange to have my car towed to a garage."

"Then you will be without a car until yours is repaired."

"I'll use the station wagon."

"What if Aunt Veronica is at the château?"

"I shall accuse her of causing our accident."

"But you can't. We are not really certain. It looked like her in the car. She had on a gray dress I've seen before. And the car was exactly like Gloria's. But it could have been someone else."

"The car was a blue Citroën. She was in Gloria's car. I happened to know it was a special paint job. There isn't another car of that particular blue in existence."

"But Gloria was not well when I left this morning."

"All the easier for Veronica to take her car. Besides, she will have recovered by the time we get there, at last sufficiently for me to talk to her."

"But if Aunt Veronica won't let you see her alone?"

"I shall arrange for that."

"I wonder if I should cable or call Mr. Graylock. He told me to if I discovered anything."

"No. I don't trust him. He may have been responsible for the whole thing."

"Oh! But he wouldn't! I'm sure he wouldn't do anything like that."

"Then you don't know him as well as I do."

"Was he there when the child was born?"

"I don't think so. It wasn't expected until six weeks later."

"Then maybe someone else? Aunt Veronica, for instance?"

"Aunt Veronica does not stand to gain anything if Gloria dies without an heir. Her father does."

"But she married again. Wouldn't her husband — ?"

"Her husband has been removed, as I was, but probably in a different way."

I could feel a chill gripping me. "You don't think — ?"

"That Preston has been murdered?"

"Oh, Paul, no!" I grabbed his arm, and he had to support me, because my knees were giving way.

Holding me with his strong arms, he said,

"Forgive me. That was brutal of me. You were in love with him."

"How did you know?"

"Gloria told me."

"I used to be. I'm not any more. But I wouldn't want him to be —"

"Don't worry. *Monsieur* Graylock is too subtle for murder."

"What do you mean by that?"

"He uses more prolonged torture — like separating two people in love, for instance."

"I see what you mean. But he never showed that side of himself in the office."

"That is how he shows his diabolical cleverness. He wouldn't dare act that way in business."

"I can't believe he is that way at any time."

"All you have to do is look at what he has done to his daughter."

I had no answer to that, and after a moment of silence between us, Paul said, "We will go over to my place before going to the château. Marie will give us lunch. It is better for us not to be seen together in a public place."

We walked back to the main street of the town, found a garage, and Paul arranged to have his car picked up and repaired. A man drove us to Paul's villa, letting us out at the gates. Paul told Marie we were there, and we sat on the terrace and had cinzano while she fixed lunch for us.

I wanted to know more about Paul, so I turned

the conversation to him by asking, "Do you do much painting?"

He said, "Yes. That is how I met Gloria. We were both going to the Sorbonne. I met her at a party in Paris."

"What was she studying?"

"Languages. When she studied. She wasn't too interested."

"And how long did you know each other before getting married?"

"About six months. Then I brought her down to my château at *Fleur-sur-Mer*. It was mine at that time." His mouth twisted in a rueful smile.

"Did you and Gloria live there long before her father came over?"

"About a week. As soon as Gloria cabled him and told him she was married, he flew right over."

"And you had never met him before?"

"No. Consequently I did not know what to expect."

"Gloria hadn't spoken about her father to you?"

"Very little. Nor had she given me any inkling that she had money. At the Sorbonne she was just one of the gang, wearing beatnik clothes, hanging around the cheap *bistros* where the Americans went — most of them getting along on what you Americans call a shoestring."

"When did you discover she was rich?"

"When her father arrived. He immediately took control of the château, ordered the servants about, and treated me as if I were one of them. Then Aunt Veronica arrived, and Gloria and I began to have trouble. We were never left alone. Her father kept telling her I was a fortune hunter, an impoverished French nobleman, and that we were, in his words, 'a dime a dozen,' which of course wasn't true. I fell in love with Gloria because she was so gay, so carefree, so beautiful. We were happy together until he came."

"Forgive me for prying, but you must have some money yourself if you had inherited the château."

He shrugged. "I have some. But we French have had to learn to, as you say, get along on the shoestring. There is also a small exporting business of perfumes. I own some property over in *Grasse,* where perfumes are made. And I sell my paintings in Paris."

"Then why did you sell Mr. Graylock the château?"

He shrugged. "One reaches a point when nothing seems to matter any more. I was losing my wife, the only girl I had ever loved. Even *she* began accusing me of marrying her for her money; she told me she was going to leave me and return to America. By then she was pregnant and I did not want my child to be born anywhere but in France. One thing followed another until we made a bargain. I would sell the château to *Monsieur* Graylock and go away if Gloria would live there and bring up our child as a Frenchman."

"That was a hard bargain."

"*Monsieur* Graylock knows how to make a hard bargain."

"So Gloria had the child at the château, but when it did not live, she no longer felt she had to stay?"

He sighed. "That is right."

"I hope you got a good price for the château. It is a very beautiful place."

"I got a very good price. That is how I was able to buy this place. As for the château being beautiful, it is in many ways. In other ways, it has too many unhappy memories for me. With my mother and my father gone, I was all alone there with just the servants." He shrugged again. "Not a very pleasant life for a young boy."

"You do not have any other relatives?"

"No. We were a small family. And the war took them all."

"And when you left the château?"

"I went down to South America. It was the most distant place I could think of. And I did some perfume business down there. Also, it was a good place to paint. But I felt as if I had lost the world — the girl I loved, my child that was to be born, and the home of my ancestors."

"But you could have kept the château if you had really wanted to."

"Yes, I could have kept it. But *monsieur* wanted it very badly. It would be to him — what you call a status symbol. So he went to work on me." For a moment there was silence between us; then he said, "That makes me sound like a weakling, doesn't it?"

"Not exactly. You're human, and you were really all alone except for Gloria."

"That's right. But if I had it to do over again, I would fight it out. Perhaps that is because I am older. I am a man now. Then I was a boy, even though it was only three years ago. I grew up on the way from France to South America. It can happen overnight, you know."

I touched his arm. "I am sorry, Paul. But maybe it isn't too late for you to regain all that you lost three years ago."

"Maybe it isn't," he said thoughtfully. "Only now I don't seem to want it any more. That is, I no longer want Gloria the way I did then; and the château, it is too big. I am happy in my new villa, here in the valley."

"And the child, if he turns out to be yours?"

His jaw tightened. "*Him* I shall fight for, right into the highest courts."

"Would the Graylock family dare to oppose you if you could prove they did what we suspect?"

"I don't know. If the mother was duped, as I was, I don't know."

"Would you remarry Gloria if she divorced Mark?"

"I might, to get the child, but not because I love her, the way I did in the beginning. If I ever marry again for love, it will have to be a different kind of girl; a girl who has had to fight her own way in the world and knows what it is all about." He gave me a long quizzical look, and I found myself blushing.

"If you remarried Gloria, wouldn't you have to take on Mr. Graylock and Aunt Veronica again?"

His lips tightened. "That would not do. And we would live here, in my villa. And I would be the boss!"

"It is none of my business," I said, "but somehow I don't think it would work any better the second time than it did the first."

He sighed. "I suppose not." Then he said, "I wonder if Mr. Graylock knows his brother-in-law has come to life and is hiding out somewhere in the château?"

"I think if he did, he would have told me when he asked me to come down."

"He was very upset about the maid, Janine."

"How was she killed?"

"You were not told?"

"No. Just that she was killed under peculiar circumstances."

"Then that is enough for you to know. The truth would only upset you more."

We had a pleasant though quiet lunch on the terrace by the garden. Neither of us felt like making conversation while we were eating, and Marie served us efficiently and quietly. Afterward we drove over to *Fleur-sur-Mer*. When we reached the bottom of the hill, Paul said, "Do you mind walking from here? I would like to reach the top of the hill quietly, not with the sound of an approaching car to warn them of our arrival. I'll leave the car at the garage here. Besides, the station wagon is too big to take up that hill."

When he drove into the garage, I didn't see Gloria's little blue Citröen standing where it had yesterday. I called it to Paul's attention, and he asked the attendant, "Is *madame* out in her car this morning?"

The attendant said, "The older *madame;* not the younger one."

Paul and I looked at each other, and he got out of the station wagon and came around and helped me out.

When we started walking up the hill, I realized how very tired I was from all the walking I'd done before lunch. But I didn't say anything. On the way up, we met only a few children, and I was glad of that. When we were negotiating the cobblestones of the *Place,* I asked, "Was that your church?" I nodded toward the simple building with its open bell tower.

He said, "No. It is a Catholic church. But the priest and I are very good friends. He lives in that small house back of the church. And the church is always open. If you ever need help, go to him."

"What is his name?"

"They call him Father John. He is quite an old man now."

"That church bell has great carrying power," I remarked. "This morning when I was walking over to your place, I could hear it way down at the end of the village."

He said, "Yes. Church bells in this country are made to carry far, so everyone in the village can hear them."

Chapter Nine

When we went through the archway into the courtyard of the château, everything was quiet and there was no one in sight. Paul tried the front door, and it opened. Quietly we entered. The trickling of the fountain at the entrance was the only sound. Paul took my arm as we went up the few steps to the large foyer. We walked over to the drawing room on the left. Gloria was sitting on the sofa, her head back, her eyes closed. She was wearing a soft blue negligee, and her fair hair was in disarray.

I said, "Gloria."

She opened her eyes languidly. When she saw me she began to whimper. "I feel awful!" she cried. "I had such a bad dream last night, and then this morning I couldn't find you."

I went and sat down beside her and took one of her hands. "Have you had anything to eat?" I asked her.

"Eat?" The word seemed to surprise her.

"Breakfast? Lunch?"

"I don't think so." She looked around the room. There was a bewildered expression in her blue eyes. Then she saw Paul. "In my dream," she said, "I called you, but you didn't come." It was an accusation rather than a statement.

He came closer to where we sat on the sofa. "If I had been there, I would have come," he said quietly. Even though he had said he no longer loved her, he was at least compassionate. He asked, "Where is Aunt Veronica?"

"I don't know," Gloria whispered. "She didn't come either. No one came, and I was all alone." She began to cry silently, but Paul made no effort to comfort her. Instead he said, "I am going out to the kitchen."

After he'd left the room, I asked Gloria, "Do you want me to help you get dressed? It is afternoon, you know."

She looked at me blankly. "Do I know you?" she asked.

I said, "Of course. I'm Carol Benson. I'm your friend. Remember?"

She thought for a moment, then nodded. "Yes. You are my friend. You slept in my room one night, and in the morning I felt so good." She sighed. "So good," she repeated.

I said, "Yes. And we went over to Saint Paul for lunch. Remember that?"

She smiled. "Yes, I remember. And there was a little boy. Paul's little boy." Suddenly she sat up stiff and straight. "Paul's little boy!" she cried. "I'll kill him!"

I gripped her hand tightly. "No, you won't."

She looked at me questioningly for a moment, and I held her eyes with mine. Then she sighed and went limp, leaning back against the sofa.

"No," she said. "No, I guess not. Paul was my husband. He loved me. No one else ever loved me. But Paul did."

"Your father loves you," I said.

"No, he doesn't. He never did. He didn't even love my mother. He just loves money. Money, *money*, MONEY!" She screamed it. "I *hate* it!" She was tense again.

Paul came in with a tray. On it was a cup of steaming coffee, a glass percolator, half full, and a chicken sandwich. He said, "Celeste says she tried to get her to eat, but she wouldn't." I got up, cleared a small table and moved it in front of Gloria. He put the tray down, then sat beside her. "Drink this coffee," he said.

"I don't want it," she whined.

"Do as I tell you! Drink it!" he said sternly.

She looked up at him and smiled. "Yes, Paul," she said, leaned over and picked up the cup. But her hand was shaking so she couldn't hold it, and it banged back onto the saucer, slopping the coffee.

Paul picked up the cup and held it to her lips, and without protest she began to drink; small sips at first, then larger swallows. When she had finished the cup, Paul refilled it from the percolator. "Now eat the sandwich with this one," he said, giving her the plate with the sandwich on it.

She obeyed him like a child, and like a child seemed grateful for the attention. As Paul guided her hands, he said to me, "You go pack while I'm doing this."

I said, "No. I can't leave her like this. Aunt Veronica —"

"What about Aunt Veronica?" she said, and, turning, I saw her standing in the doorway. She was wearing the gray dress, and she had her purse under her arm. She looked warm, as if she'd walked up the hill.

I stared at her, frightened, or rather startled by her sudden appearance. She gave me a speculative look, then turned her attention to Paul. "What are *you* doing here?" she demanded, coming into the room.

"What *you* should be doing," he told her, and held the coffee cup to Gloria's lips.

Aunt Veronica flung her purse on a chair. "What do you mean by that?" Her teeth were bared, and her dark eyes were flashing.

"Trying to get Gloria out of the drugged state she is in."

"Drugged state? What do you mean?"

Did I imagine it, or was there a momentary look of fear in her eyes?

Paul said, "Just what I say. Someone is keeping this girl drugged so she can't function properly."

Aunt Veronica took a menacing step toward him. "Get out!" she cried. "Get out of here, and don't you ever come back!"

He had finished feeding Gloria, and he stood up and walked to meet the irate woman. "I will go when I am ready," he told her, "and not one moment before."

She looked at him in amazement. "How *dare* you!"

He chewed at his moustache for a moment, then said, "I can understand why you are upset at finding Carol and me here. But it just so happens that your murderous trick on the Saint Paul road only succeeded in smashing my car a little."

She glared at him. "What on earth are you talking about? I haven't been anywhere near Saint Paul in years, and I haven't left the château since I arrived over a week ago."

Paul glanced at her purse lying on the chair where she had flung it. "You go around the château carrying your purse?" he said. "And if you weren't out in Gloria's blue Citröen, who was? It wasn't in the garage a while back, and as you can see, Gloria is in no condition to have been out driving it this morning."

Her hands clenched and her lips tightened. "You have made several very incriminating accusations, young man. If you do not leave here at once, I shall call the police."

He looked down at her the way a Great Dane might look down at a toy poodle. "That might be a good idea," he said. "A police investigation might uncover a lot of things that I would like to have explained."

She sniffed with her nose, and her mouth contorted. "We had a police investigation here only last week," she said. "They did not find out anything."

"Only a dead woman."

"That had nothing to do with us."

"Didn't it?"

She glared at him for a moment, then with an angry, "Oh!" she turned, grabbed up her purse and stalked out of the room.

To me Paul said softly, "Watch where she goes."

I went to the door into the foyer and saw her going up the stairs. I nodded to Paul and pointed upward.

He said, "Stay there and keep watch while I talk to Gloria."

I nodded again and held my ground. Paul moved the table aside and sat down beside Gloria, who, I was glad to see, looked a little better. There was intelligence in her eyes again, and she was no longer so limp.

Paul took her hand and looked into her face. "Now listen carefully," he said to her as if he were speaking to a child. "This may upset you, but it is very important."

She leaned closer to him and nodded.

"Can you understand what I am saying to you?" Paul asked her.

She said, "Yes, Paul. I feel better."

He said, "All right. It is about our baby."

She shook her head, and tears came to her eyes. "No," she said. "I don't want to talk about that."

"You must," Paul told her. "It is very necessary. Now then, do you remember what kind of clothes you had for it?"

"Clothes? Why?"

"Would you be able to recognize any of his clothes if you saw them?"

She looked up into his eyes beseechingly. "His little clothes were very beautiful," she said. "They were all handmade. Janine made them. And she helped me make some of them. I had never done any sewing before, but I made a dress. It was a beautiful dress. White silk. And I did some embroidery on the front of it. White flowers with tiny blue dots at the centers and —"

Tears were running down her cheeks now, and for a moment she couldn't go on. But Paul encouraged her. "Yes," he said. "And would you recognize the dress if you saw it?"

She nodded. "Yes, I remember. I pricked my finger with the needle. It bled. I got blood on the dress. But it was on the inside. I was hemming it, and Janine said it didn't matter because it wouldn't show."

There was no sound from the second floor, so I presumed Aunt Veronica had gone into her room. I had stood there listening to the conversation between Gloria and Paul, but I couldn't help interrupting at that point. I said, "It might not be that particular dress, Paul."

Gloria looked at me questioningly but didn't say anything. Paul said, "I realize that. But if everything was handmade, perhaps there was something to remember about each piece."

It was a very perceptive remark from a man. I sometimes make dresses for myself, and with each one there is something that I have trouble with, or something that is a little different from the pattern, that makes it uniquely distinctive. No other dress could ever turn out just like it. Not only that; I could never duplicate the dress, even myself. I could use the same pattern, same material, but each dress would have some little thing different about it. It is even that way with dresses that are made wholesale.

Gloria asked, "Why are you asking me these questions, Paul?"

He turned away from her and lit a cigarette. "I was just wondering," he said. "Did you keep the clothes after — ?"

Gloria said, "Yes. I kept them. They were all I had to keep." Her voice mumbled on the last few words.

Paul asked, "Where are they?"

"I took them home with me. They are in my bureau in the Long Island house."

Paul's brow furrowed, and he examined his cigarette. "Then they are not here."

"No," Gloria said. "But I remember each and every piece." She leaned her head back against the sofa. "I could describe each piece to you." She sighed, and tears ran unchecked down her cheeks. "They were so pretty," she whimpered. "Even the diapers; Janine embroidered little flowers on the corners." She began to cry. "And you were not here to see them," she accused him.

Paul gave her hands a gentle pat; then he

jumped up and strode over to a window. To me he said, "You don't have to keep guard any longer, Carol. I think I've found out what I wanted to know."

I left the doorway and sank down in the nearest chair. And not a moment too soon, because my knees were beginning to feel awfully strange. For several moments there was silence in the room. Then, all of a sudden, an idea struck me. "Paul," I said, "the doctor, the one who attended her at birth. Wouldn't he have had to sign a death certificate, or make a record of it somewhere?"

He swung around and looked at me. "Of course," he said. "Why didn't I think of that before?" He blackened his cigarette in an ash tray and strode over to Gloria, kneeling down beside her. "Gloria, who was your doctor?" he asked her. "When the baby was born? Was it Doctor Gautier?"

She shook her head. "No. He was away. The baby came so early. It was not expected for another six weeks."

"Then who was the doctor?" Paul persisted.

She looked bewildered. "I don't know. Someone Aunt Veronica got. I was so sick I don't remember much about it, and there wasn't time to get me to a hospital."

I went over and sat down beside her. "Do you remember what he looked like?" I asked, my heart hammering at twice its normal speed.

She shook her head. "All I remember is that —

wait a minute. It was all so hazy. It was like being in a dream. He was big. And he had light hair, I think."

"Yes, yes," I urged. "Anything else?"

She put her hands to her temples. "Let me think. There was something else. I remember — I remember something else. I think he had a square-cut beard."

Chapter Ten

Paul was reluctant to leave me at the château, but he had to. There was no use having a knockdown drag-out fight with Aunt Veronica. She would never let him stay, and I couldn't leave Gloria. My conscience wouldn't let me.

As Paul went out, he asked me to see him to the door, which I did. He opened the door, then said, "Remember, if you need help, go over to Father John."

"But suppose I shouldn't be able to leave the château?"

He sighed and took hold of my arm, giving it a squeeze. "Sleep in Gloria's room tonight and barricade the door."

"If she will let me."

"She *must* let you."

"If I could only trust the servants, at least."

He looked surprised. "Can't you?"

"Not to help in an emergency. I told you about the other night when I screamed."

He looked worried. "They were all trustworthy when I lived here. And they are the same ones."

An idea occurred to me. "Did you see any of the people who rented the château during the three years the Graylocks were back in the States?"

"No, I didn't know it had been rented. I was in South America until a couple of months ago. When I returned, I bought my place down in the valley, and I was busy getting it fixed up. I did not come up here at all. Then I saw a copy of *Paris Soir* over in Nice, and there was an announcement of Gloria's arrival in Paris on her honeymoon. So I went up. I *had* to see her." He shrugged. "You were there at our meeting, at the party in the *Crillon*. It wasn't very successful."

I said, "No, it wasn't. But what I am getting at is: has the man we fear been living here all the time? If so, he must have a confederate to bring him food, and it must be one of the servants, or some of the people who rented the château."

His eyes showed worry. "Celeste I trust. And *Jacques*. And I trusted Janine. She was like a mother to me after I lost my own mother. As to *Madame Fouchette,* I wouldn't be too sure of her. She was never too pleasant, and she was always jealous of Janine."

"What about Philippe?"

"He is all right. Or was."

"Do I dare question any of them?"

"Three years ago I would have said yes, unquestionably. Now I do not know. Everything is so different. Even honest servants can be bought sometimes, when their security and jobs depend on it. And there aren't too many jobs around like the ones they have here."

I was standing with my back to the foyer, and I noticed Paul look toward the stairs. He let go of my arm and said, "Well, I'll see you and Gloria some time tomorrow," and started out the door. Under his breath he muttered, "Here comes Aunt Veronica."

I watched him cross the courtyard and go through the arch to the *Place*. He went around the fountain and over to the church. I closed the door. When I started up the steps at the left of the fountain, I saw Aunt Veronica entering the drawing room. Quickly I followed her. I didn't want Gloria to be alone with her even for a moment.

When I entered the room, the woman was standing in front of Gloria, and the girl gave the impression of cowering. To let them know I was there, I said, "Paul has gone."

Aunt Veronica turned to me. The look on her face frightened me, but I knew I must not let her see that. She said, "I want you to keep away from that man, Carol. Understand me? He is not welcome in this house."

To my surprise, Gloria said, "This house, as you call it, happens to belong to me, and I will give the orders in it."

Without turning from me, her aunt said, "You shut up. The place belongs to your father."

"It was bought with my money." It was the first time I had heard Gloria stand up for her rights.

Aunt Veronica turned to her then. "It is in

your father's name," she said. "*I* saw to *that*. You are too incompetent to own property."

Watching Gloria, I saw the fight go out of her. She began to wilt, put her head against the back of the sofa and closed her eyes. I went and sat down beside her.

For a moment Aunt Veronica stood watching us; then she walked over and sat down in a chair near us. "Now then, Carol," she said, "what was that about an accident on the Saint Paul road?"

I should have realized she would quiz me about that the first chance she got, but I was totally unprepared for it at that moment. I quickly decided to be truthful about it. I said, "Paul and I were driving over to Saint Paul, and just as we were rounding that sharp curve before getting to the village, a blue Citröen, like Gloria's, raced up behind us, whizzed by and cut in front of us. To keep from hitting the car and sending it and us over the side, Paul rammed his car into the hill and smashed the front of it."

"And is that how you got that lump on your forehead?"

I had forgotten about that and put my hand up to explore. I touched a very sore lump and couldn't help wincing. I said, "Yes. My head hit the windshield."

"What were you doing in Paul's car, going to Saint Paul?" she demanded. She was sitting very straight in her chair, and her hands were clenching the arms of it. I decided to lie to that question. "I was taking a walk along the main street, just at the foot of the hill, and Paul came along. He saw me, stopped, and said he was on his way to Saint Paul and did I want to go along?" I tried to be nonchalant and managed a smile and a shrug. "He bribed me by promising to buy me a drink at the inn."

Keeping my eyes on Aunt Veronica's face, I could see she didn't know whether or not to believe me. Deciding to push my luck, I said, "It *was* you who cut us off, wasn't it?"

She looked at me speculatively for a moment, and if I ever saw murder in anyone's eyes, there was murder in hers at that moment. Then I could see her making a decision. She was going to use the same strategy I had used, viz., tell the truth — or part of it. She said, "I didn't realize it was you and Paul in the car. I was driving over to Saint Paul in Gloria's car, and there was a car in front of me that was poking along. I managed to pass it on that curve, which, I admit, was a silly thing to do, but I didn't realize I had caused an accident. I got past all right, and I knew I had cleared the car. Perhaps I should offer to pay for the damages to Paul's car."

"Won't Gloria or Paul's insurance pay for that?"

She knew I was challenging her, but she was equal to that. "Perhaps," she agreed. "But why were you wandering around the town at that time of the morning? Why weren't you here with Gloria?"

"She was still sleeping when I left. I had

planned on getting back within a short time. I am used to walking a lot. I need the exercise."

Beside me, Gloria sighed. "I think I'll go upstairs and get dressed. Will you help me, Carol?"

I said, "Of course," and together we got up from the sofa and walked to the door. Before going into the foyer, Gloria said to her aunt, "You lied, you know. You said you had not been away from the château since you arrived here a week ago."

"Mind your own business," Aunt Veronica snapped. I didn't even bother to excuse myself to her as I walked in front of her. She just sat there and watched us leave the room.

As soon as we got up to Gloria's room, she shut the door and turned to me. "Were you really just walking along when you met Paul?"

I decided she should know the truth, so I said, "Let's sit down, and I will tell you the whole story."

She sank down in an easy chair by the window, and I sat down near her. "No," I said, "I walked all the way over to Paul's place to ask his help."

"His help. I don't understand."

"Well, it's time you did." I decided to be a little brutal, to give her what could be called a shock treatment. "Somebody is keeping you drugged, Gloria. I think you should know."

She sighed. "I suppose those pills I take —"

"Those and something more." I told her about the man with the square-cut beard; how I had awakened the other night and found him bending over me with the hypodermic needle in his hand; how that morning, I had examined her arm and discovered the tiny red mark. She looked at her arm and saw it herself. Fright came into her blue eyes, making them seem twice their size. "That must happen to me every night," she said. "That is why I have those bad dreams and why I feel so awful in the mornings. The night you slept here with me, he didn't get at me. And in the morning I felt so good."

"Has that happened to you at home, in your father's house on Long Island?"

"No. But I have been taking pills ever since —"

I knew she meant ever since she had lost her baby. I asked, "And where do you get the pills? Does a doctor prescribe them for you?"

"No. My father gets them for me from one of his clients."

This surprised me, and I wondered which client would be so unethical. I asked, "Do you know any of the people who rented the château while you were back in the States these last three years?"

"No. My father handled all that. Sometimes he would let clients use it. And sometimes friends of Aunt Veronica's rented it. A couple of times she came over for a week or so."

"And the servants were kept on?"

"Oh, yes."

"Then that man, whoever he is, could have

been here all the time?"

"I suppose so."

"But why does he hide? Could he be your aunt's husband?"

"Oh, no. He has been dead for years, ever since the end of the Second World War."

"Perhaps he isn't dead."

She shivered. "If it's Uncle Einer, he'd *better* hide. If my father ever found out he was here —"

"Doesn't your father like him?"

"Oh, no! He hated Uncle Einer. I've heard him rave about his being a dirty Nazi. He would never let him stay here. I'm sure of that."

"Then that could be the reason he is hiding."

"If he is here, my aunt must know it."

"Yes, she must. As a matter of fact, I saw a picture of him on her dresser. Haven't you seen it?"

She shook her head. "Does she know you saw it?"

"Yes. She caught me looking at it. He is rather nice-looking. About her age. Graying light hair, and the square-cut beard."

"What did she do when she saw you looking at the picture?"

"She said it was her husband, who was dead, and that she had loved him very much. Then she put the picture in a drawer of her dresser."

"And you're sure it was the man with the square-cut beard?"

"Oh, yes."

"Then it must be a recent picture. I mean, if it was a picture taken before he was supposed to have died, he wouldn't have the square-cut beard. He would be smooth-shaven. And he would be much younger." She began to look worried. "If he is here, I'm scared. He was supposed to have had something to do with German atrocities during the war."

"Then that would be reason enough for him to hide out. If he was caught, he would be arrested and tried, as the rest of them have been."

She nodded.

I said, "Gloria, you must let me sleep here with you tonight. We'll barricade the door, and no one will be able to get in to harm you."

Tears began to run down her cheeks. "Carol, you're wonderful. I don't know how to thank you."

"Don't try. Come on now; let's get you dressed." I decided not to tell her about Paul's and my visit to the orphanage. She'd had enough for one day. And there was no use getting her hopes up. It was too tenuous a thing to count on.

When she was dressed for dinner, she said she would like to rest for a while, so I left her in an easy chair by the window and went along to my room to bathe my sore head and change my own clothes for dinner. As I walked along the hall and passed Aunt Veronica's room, the door was open, and I glanced in to see if she had replaced the picture on top of the dresser. She hadn't. I decided it must have been an oversight on her part that it had been there before.

Chapter Eleven

I wanted very much to go to the orphanage with Paul the following day but didn't see how I was going to manage it. Then something happened that solved my problem nicely. That evening after dinner, which Gloria and I had eaten alone, as Aunt Veronica did not come down, Paul called. The phone was on a small table in the foyer just outside the drawing room, and as far as I knew it was the only instrument in the château. Gloria said, "Would you answer it, Carol, please?"

I said, "Yes," put down the magazine I was looking at and went out into the foyer. When I heard Paul's voice, my heartbeat quickened, and I realized I would have to watch myself. He was beginning to mean too much to me. He said, "Carol?"

Trying to keep my voice calm, I said, "Yes. How did you know it was I?"

He laughed. "I recognized your voice. It is a very pleasant voice. I like it."

Tiny thrills crept over me. I said, "Thank you. Do you want to speak to Gloria?"

He said, "No. The reason I called is that the Saint Paul police saw my wrecked car being towed into the garage, and they called me and wanted to know what had happened. I should have reported the accident as soon as we reached the town, but I — well, as you know, I had other things on my mind."

I said, "Yes. I understand."

"*Bien*. Now they are very annoyed at me and want you and me to be at the *Préfecture* at ten tomorrow morning to make a report. Can you manage that?"

"I'll try."

"I'm afraid it is an order, from the *Préfecture*, of course. It is just a formality. We only have to tell them exactly what happened, and afterward I can go to —"

"I want to go with you," I said, keeping my voice low so no one in the château could hear me.

He said, "*Oui*. We will do that. Can you be at the bottom of the hill by nine-thirty in the morning? I will pick you up. I will be driving my station wagon."

I said, "All right. Do you want to speak to Gloria now?"

He hesitated. "No, I don't think so. We have nothing to discuss. But you'd better tell her about us having to go to the *Préfecture*."

"I will. And, Paul, will we have to tell them that we know who caused the accident?"

"I do not believe so. It would be better not to."

"I guess you're right. Good night. I'll be at the foot of the hill by nine-thirty."

When I returned to the drawing room Gloria asked, "Who was it?"

"Paul. The *Préfecture* over in Saint Paul wants to see us at ten tomorrow to get a report on the accident."

"Oh? Paul didn't report it right away?"

"No. He just didn't think of it."

"Will you tell them about Aunt Veronica?"

"Paul does not think it will be necessary."

"That's good. She'd probably lie, anyway, if they questioned her."

I didn't reply to that.

Later, when we went up to bed, Gloria didn't argue about my sleeping in her room. I think she was glad to have me. We barricaded the door by putting a table in front of it, the table with the heavy paperweight on it, so if the table was pushed over the paperweight would fall off with a crash. We had a good night's sleep, and if anyone tried to get into the room I didn't hear him. In the morning the table was just as it had been when we went to bed. Also, Gloria looked better. She had taken her pills before going to bed, but thanks to the barricaded door, nothing had been added to affect her.

We breakfasted on the back terrace, and when I started to leave for my appointment with Paul, Gloria said, "If you and Paul were going anywhere but to the police, I'd come along. But seeing it was my aunt who caused the accident, I'd better keep out of it. I'd be tempted to squeal on her, just for fun."

I laughed a little. "You wouldn't be so mean!"

"Wouldn't I? You don't know me. I can be an awful little stinker when I want to be."

I gave her hand a pat and got up from the table. She looked at me for a moment, taking in the yellow ribbon-knit dress I had chosen to wear and the large flower-embroidered straw purse I was carrying. I had tied a yellow scarf around my head to keep my hair in place, and I hoped I looked nicely.

Gloria thought I did. She said, "You are a knockout in that dress."

"Thanks."

She surveyed me critically. "Just don't get too chummy with Paul. He's mine."

There was a momentary glitter in her blue eyes, and I felt a chill slide up my back. It was on the tip of my tongue to say, "But you are married to Mark," but I knew it would only worsen what was already a sticky situation. Instead I said, "Don't worry. I'm not Paul's type."

She shrugged. "You wouldn't have been three years ago. But he has changed."

Remembering what he had said to me while we were having lunch the day before, I didn't reply. I merely said, "Well, I'd better get started. I don't think it's a good idea to be late when you have a date with the *Préfecture*."

"Will you be back for lunch?"

"I should think so."

"Bring Paul."

"Would that be wise? Aunt Veronica — ?"

She sighed. "I suppose not. Well, give him my love."

"*That* I will do," I said, and hurried away before she could say anything else.

Paul was waiting for me at the bottom of the hill. When he saw me, he leaned over and opened the door of the station wagon for me, and I got in, happy to be beside him again.

His welcoming smile was heart-warming. *"Bon jour,"* he said. "You look like a spring daffodil."

I laughed and felt such a surge of happiness that I had all I could do to keep from leaning over and kissing his cheek. But I slapped myself down by saying, "Gloria sent you her love."

Instantly his pleasant smile disappeared. "She did?" he said, and started the car.

"On the way over," he said, "I had an idea in the middle of the night. I decided it would be a good idea to write down the conversation we had with Gloria yesterday about the baby clothes. I could remember it word for word, and I got up and typed it out. I have a small portable typewriter. With it — the description Gloria gave of the baby clothes — all written down, I can let Mother Jennifer read it before I open the package. In a way — well, it might help to establish my claim on the boy."

"I think that is an excellent idea. And perhaps we had better both sign it."

"We will." Then he began to smile. "You had

better watch out, or you will be accused of being his mother."

I felt my face flushing and moved uneasily in my seat. When I didn't answer him, the smile disappeared from his face and he said, "If you had been, how different my world would be." He reached a hand out to me, and I met it with one of mine. "Oh, Carol!" he said tensely. "If things ever get straightened out —"

He was stopping before the police station now and needed both his hands to attend to the car, and I didn't feel his remark called for an answer from me. But in my heart I answered it. If ever — I thought. How wonderful it would be.

The police did not keep us long. It was merely a matter of routine. They had to keep their records straight. We both said the accident had happened so quickly we hadn't seen who had caused it; we had been too involved in our own survival to notice. We didn't believe the driver of the other car realized there had been any accident to us.

They accepted our explanation, and we were glad to get back out to the station wagon and be on our way to the orphanage.

The nun who opened the door for us was the same one who had brought little Paul to us the day before. She ushered us into the cheerless sitting room and said Mother Jennifer would see us in a few minutes.

Paul asked, "Did you find the clothing?"

The sister said, *"Oui, monsieur."*

"Is it in a package?"

"Oui, monsieur."

"Leave it that way until I can speak with Mother Jennifer."

The nun said again, *"Oui, monsieur."*

When she left us, Paul took from a pocket a piece of paper and a pen. "We will sign it now," he said. "If you cannot understand the French, I will translate it for you."

I took the pen. "It isn't necessary. I trust you." Our eyes met, and I could feel myself being kissed. Though we were several feet apart, at that moment we were very close, and there was no need for words, or even for any personal contact.

After I had signed the paper, he signed it also, leaving it on a table that was in the center of the small room.

In a moment Mother Jennifer came in. She had a package in her hands. It was wrapped in brown paper and tied with a string. *"Bon jour,"* she said pleasantly. "We have the little one's clothes." On the outside of the package there was some writing. She said, "There is a listing of the contents and the day the baby was brought to us."

"The date?" Paul asked. His face was tense now, and he looked pale.

Mother Jennifer glanced at the package. "June 2, 1964," she said.

Paul's lips tightened. "That is the right date," he said.

Mother Jennifer smiled. "That could be a coincidence. He was very tiny, new-born, and seemingly premature. We had to rush him to the hospital, where he was kept in an incubator for a couple of weeks. It is a miracle he survived." She held out the package to Paul.

He took it and placed it on the table. Then he picked up the paper we had just signed and gave it to Mother Jennifer. "Before I open the package," he said, "I want you to read this."

She took the paper, straightened her glasses on her nose and began to read it, asking, "What is it?"

Paul said, "Yesterday I talked to the child's mother. As I told you, I was out of the country when the child was born and was supposed to have died. I asked my former wife if she could describe the baby clothes to me, and she said she could. She remembered them very well. They were all handmade, and she had made some of them herself. I have written down our conversation just as it took place. This young lady was there and heard everything that was said."

Mother Jennifer glanced at my signature. "Carol Benson?" she asked.

I said, *"Oui."*

She smiled. *"Parlez-vous français?"* she asked.

"Un peu," I said. *"Pas beaucoup."*

She sat down on a chair and motioned us to take seats; then she began to read what Paul had typed out in the middle of the night.

As we waited, Paul and I avoided looking at

one another. We were both tense, and I could see Paul's hands trembling as he clasped them together.

When Mother Jennifer finished reading the paper, she leaned over and put it on the table beside the package. "You must not be disappointed if the clothing in the little package is different," she said quietly.

Paul nodded his head. Color was coming back into his cheeks. Now they were almost too red, and beads of perspiration were wetting his forehead.

Mother Jennifer said, "Shall I open the package for you?"

"*S'il vous plaît.*" Paul held out his hands to show her how they were trembling. "I don't think I could."

She nodded and opened the package with her strong, steady hands.

The paper opened, she spread out the contents of the package so we could see what was there. It contained a white silk dress, slightly yellowed with age. On it were embroidered little white flowers with blue dot centers. There was underclothing, all handmade, and a diaper with embroidery in the corner. Mother Jennifer touched the dress and turned back the hem. Near a seam were several darkened spots. They could have been blood from a pricked finger. And there was a soft white blanket bound in white satin ribbon. This also had a little embroidery in one corner, like the diaper.

No one spoke. I could feel chills running up and down my back, and my hands were like ice in spite of the fact that room was very warm.

Then Paul covered his face with his hands and began to sob; great, wracking sobs that would break your heart. Mother Jennifer and I exchanged glances. I guess I looked frightened, because she motioned to me to go with her. Quietly we got up and left the room, and she led me along the hall and into another room. "This is my office," she said. "You see I speak a leetle English. Not much."

When we were seated in her office, which contained a desk and several chairs, the usual religious pictures and a crucifix, she said, "He will feel better if we do not watch him. He has had a shock."

I nodded. "I understand." After a moment I said, "Then the child must be his."

"*Oui*. It is strong evidence. That, and the fact that they look so much alike." Then she added, "I remember his father, the child's grandfather. They all looked alike, the Thireau men."

"Will he be able to have the child?" I asked, choking back my own tears with an effort.

"Eventually. There will have to be an investigation. It will take time."

"And the ones who perpetrated the crime? For surely it was a crime to let the child's mother believe it had died."

Mother Jennifer nodded. "It was an evil thing to do. There should be some punishment."

"But how can it be proved?"

Mother Jennifer crossed herself and began fingering the rosary that hung from her waist. "We will leave that to God," she said. "God will mete out his own punishment. It is not for us to do."

I didn't quite agree with her, and I was beginning to worry about Paul. I said, "Perhaps I had better go to *monsieur* now."

"*Oui.* I will come in later."

So I got up and went along to the small sitting room. Paul had stopped crying and was fingering the tiny garments, with almost, I thought, as much reverence as Mother Jennifer fingered her rosary.

When I entered the room, he looked up. There were still tears in his eyes. I smiled at him, and he held out a hand to me. I took it and put my other hand on his shoulder. "I'm so glad, Paul," I said. "So very glad for you."

He nodded his head and squeezed my hand. He couldn't speak, and his hand was shaking. Then suddenly he turned and put his arms around me and held me close to him for a minute. When he let me go, he was able to smile. "Always believe in miracles, Carol," he said. "I never have before, but this is certainly one."

I couldn't help saying, "One you should be sharing with Gloria." Then I was sorry I'd said it, because his lips tightened and he pushed me away.

Mother Jennifer came in just then. She held

out her hands to Paul. "God bless you, my son," she said.

Paul gripped her hands. "May I see my son now?" he asked.

She shook her head. "Not yet," she said gently. "I have taken the precaution of having him transferred to another town, far from this one, for his protection."

"Oh, but — !" Paul cried.

She kept shaking her head at him. "Patience, my son," she said. "Anyone evil enough to have done this terrible thing is evil enough to do more damage. And if they think you have discovered the truth — We must be very careful until we have made our investigation."

"I see what you mean," Paul said, but he looked disappointed. "Will the police have to be called in?"

"It is the only way. But it will be handled with the utmost discretion."

Paul said, *"Oui, oui."*

Mother Jennifer let his hands go. "I would advise you to say nothing to anyone, not even the child's mother," she said. "It might endanger our discovering the truth."

He nodded. "I understand. How long will it take?"

"That we cannot predict. I am convinced the child is yours, and you shall have him as soon as the legal — what you call red tape — has been gone through. If you take him before the ones who did this terrible thing have been discovered and apprehended, you might endanger his life."

Paul's broad shoulders sagged, but he nodded his agreement.

As we started to leave, Mother Jennifer asked, "Do you want to take the clothing?"

He thought a moment, then said, "No. You keep it here, with my signed description of the things. We may have to take them into court. And they will be safer here with you."

She nodded. "That will be the better way," she said, and began wrapping up the tiny garments.

When we were outside in the station wagon, Paul said, "How about some lunch? It is after twelve."

There was nothing I would have liked better than to lunch with him, but I had to say, "Gloria is expecting me back for lunch."

He took my hand and squeezed it. "I hate to let you go," he said. "Life is beginning to be very empty without you."

I pulled my hand away. "You are just overly emotional. I understand. But, after all, you've only known me for a few days."

He smiled ruefully. "Sometimes it happens at first sight." He started the car, turned it around and drove slowly toward *Fleur-sur-Mer*.

After a while I said, "Poor Gloria. Shouldn't she be told her baby did not die? She would be so happy."

"I wonder," he said. "For a while, maybe. But somehow I can't imagine her having patience with an active small boy."

"Perhaps it would be just the therapy she needs. If losing the baby made her the way she is, wouldn't finding him make her better?"

"I'm not sure. Nor would I want to trust the child to *Monsieur* Graylock and Aunt Veronica."

"Nor would I. But if you and Gloria remarried and she and the little fellow lived with you at your villa in the valley — ?"

To my surprise, he clenched one of his hands into a tight fist and pounded the car wheel with it. Through tight lips he said, "I cannot consider that — now!"

Frightened, I didn't know what to say, and for the rest of the ride neither of us spoke again. When we reached the foot of the hill, he stopped the car. "Do you mind walking up?" he asked. "I could walk up with you, but I do not want to see any of them, feeling the way I do at this minute."

I said, "All right, Paul," opened the door beside me and got out.

Our goodbye was merely the lifting of a hand, but our eyes said all that could be said under the circumstances.

When I reached the château, Gloria and her aunt were having cocktails on the back terrace. Celeste had been watching for me and met me in the foyer. "You are to go out to the back terrace," she told me. "Lunch will be served in a few minutes."

I said, *"Merci,"* and went through the dining

room and out to where Gloria and her aunt were sitting. They didn't seem to be talking, just sitting and drinking their cocktails. They both looked up when I came out, and Gloria said, "Well, it took you long enough. Have you been at the *Préfecture* all this time?" I thought she looked sullen, but there was no sign of the depression she had been in the day before. At least I had saved her from that by sleeping in her room last night.

A pitcher of cocktails and a glass were on the table against the wall. Aunt Veronica said, "Help yourself. We're two up on you."

I poured myself a drink and sat down. I needed a drink by that time. After my first sip, I said, "The police do not move very fast, and they like to keep folks waiting. I'm sorry if I delayed your lunch."

Gloria didn't answer me, but I saw her gaze wandering over the countryside to where Paul's white villa spread out in the bright sunshine.

Aunt Veronica asked, "Did you mention me to the police?"

I said, "No. Paul did not think it necessary."

She made an angry sound. "Oh, he didn't? How nice of him!"

I met her eyes. They were hostile and frightening.

"Paul is not vicious," I said.

"See how she defends him?" Gloria asked her aunt. To which her aunt said, "Shut up!"

I sipped my drink and found my own eyes

straying over toward Paul's villa. I wondered if he was having his lunch alone at the end of his lovely garden. The whole Riviera was so lovely it was a shame the people who had the opportunity to enjoy it didn't seem to be able to. I said, "Gloria, why don't you get in touch with Mark and ask him to come back here so you can finish your honeymoon?"

Over the top of her cocktail glass, her blue eyes flashed at me. "So you can have Paul all to yourself?"

Aunt Veronica began to smile, but it was a vicious smile. "That would be nice," she said to Gloria. "You and Mark, and Carol and Paul. It would make an interesting foursome."

Gloria jumped up from her chair and threw the remaining contents of her cocktail in her aunt's face. Her aunt gasped, then with a look of terrifying hate she threw her cocktail, glass and all, at Gloria. It hit her in the mouth, and I heard the glass click as it struck her teeth, but fortunately it didn't break until it fell to the flagstones at her feet.

Celeste was just coming out with a tray of soup plates and saw what happened. She turned back into the dining room, put the tray on the dining table, returned with clean towels and wordlessly began to wipe the spilled drinks from both Gloria and Aunt Veronica, who, after venting their spite against each other, seemed to be subdued and stood like penitent children while Celeste took care of them. Then Celeste picked up the pieces of the broken cocktail glass and took them inside.

Without a word I got up, left my glass on the table and went up to my room. No one stopped me. There was no use in the three of us trying to eat lunch together as if nothing had happened.

I closed my door and sank down on the *chaise longue.* I would have to get away from the château high on the hill. I couldn't stand any more of it. I didn't want to leave Paul, though. He would need me to testify if the case of little Paul's identity went to court.

Nevertheless I packed my bags.

I would stay one more night, and then I would leave. I would go over to Nice, and from there I would cable Mr. Graylock and tell him to come at once. I couldn't very well tell him what I had discovered, because I no longer trusted him. But the women at the château were his responsibility. If he wanted to bring Mark with him, well and good. But I did not think Mark's marriage to Gloria would last much longer, no matter what else happened.

Chapter Twelve

Later in the afternoon, I decided to go downstairs. I'd finished my packing, and there was nothing else for me to do. As I passed Gloria's room, I saw her door was open. She was lying on the *chaise longue* by the window. She saw me and called me in. I went just inside the door. She said, "I'm sorry about what happened at lunch."

I said, "That's all right."

"No, it isn't. But Aunt Veronica makes me so mad. She likes to taunt me about Paul."

I said, "I'm sorry. But you don't have to worry about Paul, as far as I am concerned, because I'm leaving. I have packed my bags, and I will leave tomorrow."

She sat up straight on the *chaise longue,* and a look of fright came into her eyes. "Oh no! Don't leave me! Please!"

"Don't you think I should send for your father — and your husband?"

She closed her eyes, then opened them just a little so they were mere slits in her white face. It made her look like a cat. "No!" she said, her teeth clenched. "And if you *dare,* I'll *kill* you!" She began to get up from the *chaise longue,* and I backed into the hall.

When she saw I was frightened by her, she laughed. "You *are* a fraidy cat, aren't you?" She chuckled. "But I am only teasing. I'm a big, brave girl now, because I've just taken a couple of my pep pills. But it will wear off, and then I'll be meek little Gloria again."

I felt suddenly weak. If ever anyone needed psychiatric treatment, Gloria did. I said, "I'm going down to the drawing room. Will you come down with me?"

She sank down on the side of the bed. "Later," she said. "You go ahead."

Aunt Veronica did not join us for cocktails and dinner, so Gloria and I were alone. Neither of us had bothered to dress, and it wasn't what you would call a gay meal, although the food was delicious, as always. Whatever *Madame Fouchette*'s disposition, she was certainly an excellent cook.

After dinner, when we went into the drawing room, Gloria was restless. She hadn't taken her pill from the small gold, jewel-incrusted box at the dinner table, and I wondered if she had forgotten it because Aunt Veronica hadn't been there to urge it on her, or if she had deliberately refrained from taking it, hoping to begin to break herself of the habit. Or possibly if she had taken so many of what she called her pep pills during the afternoon, she didn't need any more for a while. I didn't dare ask.

After a while she said, "I wish we could take a walk."

"Why can't we?"

"There is no place to go."

"We could walk around the gardens."

The idea seemed to please her. "All right, let's."

So we went out the front door and walked around to the back, the way I had that first day when I had been looking for the back terrace. It was not quite dark, and the scent of the flowers was heady and pleasant. Sleepy birds were darting around before going to their nests for the night, and their twittering was companionable. Suddenly Gloria asked, "Tell me the truth, do you really like Paul?"

I almost stumbled on the rock steps. "Why, yes," I said truthfully. I wouldn't admit even to myself how much I liked him.

Gloria said, "I wish I hadn't married Mark. Then Paul and I could get married again."

Logical as it was, the idea disturbed me, even though I had presented it to Paul myself. I asked, "Why *did* you marry Mark?" I was a little ahead of her on the path, and I had to ask my question over my shoulder, rather glad that she couldn't see my face.

She didn't answer me for a moment, and I began to wonder if I had made a mistake in asking the question. But then she said, "I don't really know. My father kept bringing him to the house, and I hadn't had any fun in three years. And he was very nice. It seemed to be the line of least resistance. And I thought it would give me a chance to get away from my father and Aunt Veronica for a while."

"Why did you want to do that?" We had reached the lowest part of the garden, and there was a white-painted iron settee there. We sat down on it, and the birds twittered around us. She said, "Well, for one thing, I was awfully tired of the argument about my giving my father money to put in the agency."

"Why did he want you to do that? The agency is successful. It does not need outside money."

"Doesn't it?" She sighed. "You see, I didn't know that. He kept telling me he was in need of financial help, and it was my duty as his daughter to give it to him. But I am not his daughter. Not really. I was two years old when my mother married him. My own father had been killed in whatever war was going on at that time. I forget."

I tried not to show my surprise at that bit of information. But I began to see the plan. I said, "And your stepfather kept giving you pills?"

She was twisting her hands together in her lap. "Yes," she said. "He told me I needed them. If I didn't take them, I would have a serious nervous breakdown and have to be hospitalized."

"Didn't you have a doctor?"

"No. He said I didn't need one, that he knew how to take care of me."

I remembered Paul saying, "All you have to do is look at what he has done to his daughter." I asked, "Have you ever signed any papers?"

"No. Several times he has tried to get me to,

after I'd taken pills, but I never would. I remembered my mother saying that when she died, I was to save all the money for my children and that I mustn't let my stepfather get any of it."

"Don't you have a lawyer?"

"Just my stepfather's lawyer."

"Aren't there any relatives of your real father who could help you?"

"I don't know. My mother and I were alienated from them after my father died. They hadn't approved of my mother, because she had been an actress and they had been straight-laced New Englanders. So after my father died, they wouldn't have anything to do with us."

"That's too bad. But — well, your father must have been wealthy in his own right."

"He was. His grandfather had been a wealthy contractor, and he had left all his money to him. And that was another thing that made my father's folks mad at us. They didn't think we should get that money."

Money, I thought. I've always wished I had some of it, but here was a family, several families in fact, that had been made miserable because of it. I asked, "Does Mr. Graylock's lawyer — your lawyer — ever try to get you to sign papers?"

"No."

"Have you ever told him that your stepfather has?"

"No."

"Perhaps you should. Also, perhaps you should go to a doctor and tell him about all the different kind of pills you've been taking. Do you know what they are?"

"No. All I know is that they make me sleep so I don't think about —" The tears began to fall again. "And sometimes they pick me up, and I want to fight the world single-handed."

I said, "Well, let's walk some more." It was almost dark now, the birds had gone to their nests, and I didn't like the idea of being down at the bottom of the garden so far from the house. I didn't know what could happen to us down there, but I had reached the point where I saw potential danger everywhere.

We had just stepped up onto the terrace when something came down at us from above. A slight sound had made me look up just in time to see something dark hurtling toward us from the roof. Without saying anything, I grabbed Gloria so roughly we both tripped and fell to one side. And not a moment too soon. A large piece of stone hit the flagstones right where we had been, smashing into sharp-edged small pieces and cracking the flagstones on which it had landed. I shuddered to think what it would have done to our heads.

For a moment Gloria and I lay where we had fallen, too startled to move. I recovered first and helped her to her feet. "What *was* it?" she gasped.

I looked up at the various windows of the château but could see nothing. They were all without lights. Did I imagine it, or was there a shadow on the roof directly over us? It was too dark now for me to be sure, and in any case it disappeared instantly.

Gloria was looking down at the fragments of the thing that had nearly hit us. "It looks like a piece of the cornice from the roof," she said. "I'd better have someone come and repair it before any more of it falls off."

I pushed her over to the doors into the dining room, saying, "Or before anybody pushes another piece of it off."

The lights in the dining room were out, but the foyer was lit, and so was the drawing room beyond. Gloria said, "Oh, don't be silly! Why would anyone push a piece of cornice off on us?"

"I'm not sure," I said. "But I could give an educated guess."

She giggled. "You'll be seeing spooks next," she told me.

"I'd rather see a spook than some of the live people around here," I snapped. My nerves were beginning to feel the strain, and I no longer felt equal to combating the entire château and its strange occupants.

Chapter Thirteen

When we went upstairs to bed, Aunt Veronica's door was closed, and there was no sound from her room. Gloria asked, "Are you sleeping with me again tonight?"

"Do you want me to?"

"Yes, please."

So I undressed and bathed in my own room before going over to Gloria's. When I got there, she was waiting for me. "I just took two pills," she said. "I don't want to lie awake."

"Maybe you wouldn't. Why don't you try sometime?"

She shrugged. "What's the difference?" It was her stock excuse.

I began to feel impatient with her. "There is a lot of difference," I told her crossly. "Are you going to spend the rest of your life just half alive, the way you are now? You're young, beautiful, rich. You could have a good life, enjoy yourself."

"No, I couldn't."

"Why not?"

"Because it's too late."

"That's ridiculous!"

"Paul doesn't want me any more."

"Of course he does. Otherwise, why would he

be trying to help you the way he is?"

"Just out of decency. That's the way he is."

"Well, he won't want you the way you are now, that's for sure. He's a big strong, red-blooded man, and he needs a woman who is alive, one who can be a mate to him; not one who is letting herself be a semi-invalid!"

I guess I spoke too vehemently, letting my subconscious emotions carry me away, because she stood there staring at me in surprise, almost in fright. Then she cried, "You *are* in love with him! You want him for yourself!" Her blue eyes were blazing, and she was trembling. "Well, you're not going to get him. I'll *kill* you first!" She picked up the heavy glass paperweight from the table and advanced on me with it upraised in such a way that the snow was blizzarding over the scene within the glass sphere.

For a moment I was too surprised to move. I knew she was a sick girl, but I hadn't realized she was homicidal. I had thought it was just talk. I opened my mouth to scream, then remembered it wouldn't do me any good. And by that time I had regained my poise enough to go into action. I grabbed her wrist just as her arm was coming down at my head. With all the strength I could command, I pushed her arm to the side, knocked the paperweight from her hand so it crashed on the floor, then slapped her face, good and hard.

She gasped, stared at me blankly and then fainted, falling limply at my feet on top of the paperweight, which was still holding its private little blizzard.

I was stunned. What should I do? Should I call Aunt Veronica? Go upstairs for Celeste? The door to the room was closed, and we were alone. I knelt down beside Gloria and felt her pulse. It was beating rapidly and there were beads of perspiration on her forehead and around her mouth.

I ran into the bathroom, wet a towel with cold water and ran back and knelt beside her again, bathing her face, holding the cold wet cloth to her forehead. To tell the truth, I was scared half to death. What had I done to the girl? Suppose she died there, alone with me?

I went back to the bathroom and got a glass of cold water. I sprinkled some of it on her face, then got one arm beneath her shoulders and held the glass to her lips. Some of the water went into her mouth, but most of it ran down her neck. After a few minutes her eyelids fluttered open, she looked up at me and smiled faintly. "I don't feel good," she whimpered.

I helped her to her feet and got her over to the bed. She flopped down upon it like a rag doll. "How many of those pills did you take?" I demanded.

She sighed. "I don't remember."

Kneeling on the bed beside her, I shook her, not too gently. "Tell me!" I cried. "How many?"

Her eyes closed, and she sighed and then lay

perfectly still. I realized she was unconscious again.

The only thing I could think of to do was to get her black coffee. I opened the door and rushed into the hall, leaving the door open behind me, and ran down the stairs to the kitchen, forgetting the menace I might encounter in the halls of the château at night. But it was only ten o'clock, and the lights were still on downstairs.

I had never been in the kitchen before, but I presumed it must be back of the dining room, and of course I knew which door Celeste came through when she was serving us our food at mealtime.

I swung the door open onto a large paneled room, hung with shining copper pots and pans. Celeste and *Madame Fouchette* were sitting at a table drinking coffee. It was the first time I had seen *Madame Fouchette*. She was tall and thin, almost gaunt, and she had graying black hair and small black bird-like eyes. She glared at me with an air almost of disgust. But I had no time to worry about that. "Quick!" I cried. "I need black coffee for Gloria. She's passed out!"

Celeste jumped up. "Too many pills?" she asked, going to the large shining stove for the coffeepot. But it was nearly empty, and she said, "I'll have to make fresh."

I said, "Well, hurry, please. I'm scared. She looks terrible. I don't know how many pills she took, but she tried to kill me."

"*Oh mon dieu!*" *Madame Fouchette* cried. "I

knew she was mad! She has been ever since —"

"She isn't at all mad!" I snapped. "She is a very sick girl!" To Celeste I said, "Can't we get a doctor for her?"

"Oh no!" Celeste cried. "We would lose our jobs."

"Well, I'd like to lose this job. Do you know the phone number of Doctor Gautier?" I remembered the name of the doctor Paul had mentioned when he had been talking to Gloria about the birth of the baby. Then I decided I had to tell Paul first. He could call the doctor for me, and they could come up together. If he came also, I would feel better about everything.

I ran out to the phone in the foyer. There was a phone book in a shelf beneath the table top. I found Paul's number and got him. I cried, "Paul, it's Gloria! She's taken too many pills. She's unconscious! Bring a doctor. Quick!"

He said, "Right away. Take it easy. Give her black coffee!"

I said, "All right. But hurry!"

"I will."

I ran back to the kitchen. Celeste was waiting for the fresh coffee to perk, and *Madame Fouchette* was not too graciously fixing a tray with a cup and saucer and a napkin. I was trembling and had to sit down in a chair while we waited for the coffee. Perhaps I should have gone back to Gloria and stayed with her while the coffee was perking, but I didn't believe my legs would take me up the stairs. And by the time the coffee was ready, Paul and the doctor had arrived, together. It seemed incredible they could have gotten there so quickly.

The doctor was a small, rotund man with red cheeks, bright blue eyes, thinning gray hair and a large moustache. He carried the inevitable black bag.

"Where is she?" Paul asked.

"Up in her room."

He took the stairs two at a time, and the doctor followed as quickly as he could, with his shorter legs and additional avoirdupois. Celeste and I followed him, and *Madame Fouchette* brought up the rear, carrying the tray with the coffee, a sour look on her gaunt face.

When we reached Gloria's room, Paul was staring down at her, and the doctor was bending over her. He was examining her neck. Celeste, *Madame Fouchette* and I stood to one side waiting, all of us uneasy, and I, for one, feeling as if my heart were going to jump out of my body.

At last the doctor straightened up, and I could see Gloria's neck. It was slit from top to bottom, the cut was open, but there wasn't a drop of blood.

"*Mon dieu!*" *Madame Fouchette* cried hoarsely. "*Comme ça, Janine.*"

I looked at Paul. "What is it?" I managed to ask, but my voice was little more than a squeak.

He came over to me and put an arm around me. "Laser ray," he said. "Bloodless surgery."

"What do you mean?" I asked.

"The ray cauterizes as the knife cuts, so there is no blood. But the incision is supposed to be sutured after the operation. As far as I know, it is just in the experimental stages."

The doctor said, "This is another case for the police. There is nothing I can do. It is too late."

Aunt Veronica's door opened, and she came into Gloria's room. She was wearing a very beautiful electric blue housecoat that touched the floor. "What is going on here?" she demanded.

"Perhaps you can tell us?" Paul said, tightening his hold on me.

She walked over to the bed and looked down at her niece. It wasn't a pretty sight, even though there wasn't any blood. With a gasp, she sank to the floor in a heap. The doctor looked down at her. "She has only fainted," he said. "Perhaps it is just as well. But we must get the police."

I said, "You take care of her. I'll call the police."

Paul released his hold on me. "Would you mind?" he asked. "I think I'd better stay here."

Chapter Fourteen

I left the room and ran down the stairs. Paul called after me, "Just ask the operator for the *Préfecture* of police."

The downstairs looked vast and empty, and suddenly I realized I was the only one on that floor. Everyone else was upstairs. But there was nothing to be afraid of downstairs. The menace was upstairs. It came from the top floor, from the closed part of the château. But there might be ways to come through to this part on this floor that I did not know of.

I ran to the table against the wall of the foyer and grabbed up the receiver with my trembling hand. But the phone was dead. I jiggled the bar up and down, and then I noticed the wire was cut at the baseboard. Then all the lights went out, and from behind me a large, antiseptic-smelling hand was clamped over my mouth. The phone was taken from me and replaced on its useless cradle. Then the hand left my mouth, and two hands, as strong as iron, were placed around my throat, choking me; pressing, pressing until I couldn't breathe. Close behind me I could hear heavy breathing — the kind I had heard the night I was awakened in Gloria's room and found the man with the square-cut beard bending over me. I could feel the beard now, tickling the back of my neck.

I realized I was a goner if I didn't act quickly. Help was only a staircase away, but I couldn't let them know. And the lights upstairs must have gone out, too, because I could hear Paul's raised voice telling Celeste to get candles.

Struggling silently with my powerful assailant, I suddenly remembered something I had read about self-defense. It wasn't anything I liked doing, but it was a case of saving my life, if I could. So with all the strength born of my desperation, I kicked back and upward with one foot, hoping the heel of my shoe would land in the right spot. If it didn't the first time, I knew I wouldn't have a second chance.

But I must have made contact, because the man behind me let go of my throat, gave a groan, then began to curse in German. Or at least it sounded like cursing.

As soon as I was released, I ran toward the front door, feeling my way carefully down the steps beside the fountain. I could hear the man muttering and groaning back of me in the foyer. Then I was out the door, running through the courtyard of the château, through the stone arch, into and across the *Place,* slipping on the cobblestones. There was no place I could think of to run to but the church. Paul had told me to go to Father John. If I could just get inside the church before the man who had tried to strangle me recovered enough to pursue me!

I had almost made it to the church door when I heard heavy footsteps following me. Glancing around, I saw it was the man I feared. But he couldn't walk too fast because of the damage I had done him. He had on the white doctor's coat, but it was too dark for me to see his face. I didn't have to, to know who he was.

Quickly I ran into the dimly lit church. I called, "Father John!" But the church was empty. The old Father was probably in bed asleep in his snug little house behind the church. But I didn't know how to get to the house without going out and around. And I daren't do that.

The heavy footsteps were crossing the *Place* now. The man had seen me enter the church. In another moment he would be in the door, and I would be cornered. At the right of the entrance I saw a spiral staircase. I ran to it, climbing the narrow, twisting stairs as quickly as I could. At the top, I saw I was in the open bell tower. The bell rope was hanging down from the center. Looking up, I could see the dark shape of the bell.

Without thinking, I grabbed the rope, pulling on it with all my strength. It was hard to get the bell started, but when it once began to move and the first clang rang out over the darkness of the *Place,* it became easier. Desperately I tugged at the rope, and with frantic clangs the bell responded. It was ear-splitting, but my ears weren't my present concern. I knew the sound of the bell was going out and all around the hill and way down into the village.

The bell was making such a racket I couldn't hear whether or not my pursuer had come into the church. My one idea was to arouse the entire town. If I couldn't reach the police by phone, maybe I could reach them this way, for surely, hearing the church bell ringing so wildly in the night, everyone would come to find out why.

Then I looked down the spiral staircase and saw the head of the man I feared appear, then come closer and closer, step by step. But I kept tugging at the bell rope, my hands feeling raw and cut, my heart in my throat, choking me with its wild beating. My breath was labored, as if I were dying. Maybe I was — or would be in a moment.

I kept watching the head of the man coming up the stairs, each step bringing him closer.

Then he stopped, staggered and disappeared. Still I kept frantically pulling the bell rope. But I couldn't go on much longer. It was beginning to feel faint and dizzy.

Then I saw Paul coming up the stairs with a gun in his hand, and everything went black. . . .

I had often wondered if dying was a case of blacking out in this world and later becoming gradually conscious in another.

So when I became gradually conscious after blacking out in the bell tower and seeing Paul coming up the steps toward me with a gun in his hand, I didn't know what to expect. I wondered what the first thing would be that I would see in that other world.

I could hear movement around me, and there were voices, footsteps, and lights that seemed to shine through my closed eyelids. It was very like the world I had left. I decided the only thing to do was to open my eyes. When I did, I saw arched rafters, like those in a church. I looked around, listening. After a moment I realized I was lying on a church pew. It was hard. There was no cushion. It sounded as if dozens of people were excitedly arguing in French.

I sat up so I could see what was going on. I was in the little church in the *Place,* and there was a crowd of people in the back of the church. The doors were open, and I could see out to the *Place.* It was filled with people and vehicles. Somehow the vehicles had managed to come up the steep narrow road to the top of the hill. There was a fire engine and several police cars and an ambulance. The people consisted of men and women, some in their nightclothes, policemen, or *gendarmes,* as they call them in France, and a couple of young doctors in white who must have come with the ambulance. I didn't see a single familiar face, and if anyone knew I was there he didn't give any evidence of it.

I felt my head. There was still the sore lump where I'd hit the windshield of Paul's car yesterday, and there was a feeling of dizziness. That was all. I wondered if Paul had shot me. A careful investigation of myself showed me to be in perfect condition. Then what had happened? Had my ringing of the church bell brought all these people and vehicles?

I got to my feet and walked slowly to the back of the church. Gradually it was all coming back to me. Gloria, lying on her bed with her throat cut, but no blood anywhere. My trying to phone the police and discovering the wire had been severed. The man with the square-cut beard trying to strangle me. My flight to the church and my frantic ringing of the bell. Then the man with the square-cut beard slowly coming up the spiral stairs to the bell tower — his sudden disappearance — and Paul coming up the staircase with a gun in his hand.

A feeling of hopelessness crept over me. If Paul had meant to shoot me, why hadn't he? And if he had wanted to, I wished he had, because this way there was nothing left for me. If Paul was against me, life wasn't going to be worth living. When I lost Mark, I was able to pick myself up, dust myself off and start all over again. But if I lost Paul it would be the end.

Unnoticed, I left the church and went out to the *Place*. A group of people were looking down at something on the ground. It was the man with the square-cut beard, and he was dead. He was lying on a stretcher, and he was no longer a person to fear. The crazy thought went through my mind that I did not know what kind of other world he would become conscious in, now he had left this one.

As my eyes became accustomed to the bright lights of the vehicle headlights that were making the *Place* brighter than day, I was able to distinguish faces. Paul, looking haggard and about ten years older than he had earlier in the evening, and without the gun, was talking to a couple of policemen and a doctor from the ambulance. After a while two men lifted one stretcher with the man with the square-cut beard on it, shoved it into the ambulance and closed the doors.

Slowly and carefully the ambulance moved through the crowd, around the *Place* and through the archway to the château. It stopped at the entrance, and I saw that the doors were wide open, both of them. There were lights in the château again, and the foyer was milling with people.

Paul had followed the ambulance and entered the château with the two men in white, who were carrying another stretcher — empty.

Standing to one side, lost in the crowd of people, I wondered if I should go inside. But I was too afraid. If Paul had been going to shoot me, I had better stay away from him. Tears came to my eyes, and I whispered, "Oh no, Paul! You *couldn't!* You *wouldn't!*"

Then the men in white came out. There was a sheet-covered body strapped to the stretcher. I knew it must be Gloria, and I began to sob. I had all I could do to keep from running and touching the object on the stretcher. We had fought, and my stay at the château high on the hill had not been pleasant, but suddenly I realized I had grown fond of Gloria, and I had tried to be her friend.

I stood sobbing quietly until the ambulance had gone back through the archway and around the cobblestoned *Place*. Then, as it drove slowly down the hill, its siren wailed mournfully, like a soul disappearing into purgatory, the wailing becoming fainter and fainter until it was no longer audible.

Not until then could I bring myself to walk toward the château. I knew I would have to go in eventually and face whatever there was left to face. If Paul wanted to shoot me, let him. Like Gloria taking her pills, I thought, What's the difference?

I looked around for a familiar face. There was none. I wondered where the servants were. Where Paul was. Where Aunt Veronica was. And where Doctor Gautier was.

There was no one in the drawing room, so I went there and sank down on the sofa, and that was where Paul found me what seemed like eons later. I was half asleep, so exhausted was I, both physically and emotionally.

I heard Paul's voice say, "Carol! I've looked everywhere for you! I left you on a pew in the church."

I opened my eyes and held my breath. He didn't have the gun. I asked, "Are you going to kill me now, Paul?"

He came and sat down beside me. "Kill you? Of course not, you silly goose. Why would I kill the girl I love?"

My heart, which had been in a state of shock, suddenly began to beat normally again. I sighed and let him take my hand. "In this church, you were coming up the stairs toward me — with a gun."

He gripped my hands. "I was coming up to get you to tell you you were safe and you could stop ringing the bell. I'd just shot Meyerhoff so he couldn't reach you."

"You killed him?"

"No. I just shot him in the leg to stop him from reaching you. But he fell down the stairs and broke his neck."

"How did you know I was up in the bell tower?"

"I was just starting to come down the stairs here to get some candles from the kitchen when I saw the front door open and saw you run out. Then a man ran after you. I went to the phone and discovered the wire was cut. Then the church bell began to ring, and I remembered telling you, if you were in trouble, to go to Father John. Well, I knew that Father John would be in bed at that time of night and figured ringing the bell was your way of trying to summon help. Fortunately, I had a gun in my pocket; I had decided one would be a good thing to have when I came up here, after what had been happening."

I began to tremble, and sobs wracked my tired body. Paul took me in his arms, held me close to him and let me cry for a while. Then Celeste came into the room, asking, "Is *mademoiselle* all right?" She looked like a ghost, she was so white and scared.

Paul said, "Yes, she is all right. Would you bring us some brandy, please?"

Celeste said, *"Oui, monsieur,"* and went out. In a couple of minutes she returned with a decanter and two glasses on a tray and pulled up a small table to set them on. After I'd had a few sips of the brandy, I began to feel better. As Celeste went out of the room, she closed the door, explaining, "So no one will come in and bother you."

Paul was also sipping brandy, and from the looks of him he certainly needed it.

After a while I asked, "Where is Aunt Veronica?"

Paul gulped a big swallow of his brandy. "Up in bed. Doctor Gautier is with her, and two policemen. Also Father John. She is under sedation now. Tomorrow she will be taken to a hospital."

"A hospital?" I cried. "What happened to *her?*"

Paul put his brandy glass on the small table and lit a cigarette. His hands were trembling, and in the flame from his lighter his face looked very haggard and old. I moved closer to him and put a hand on his arm. When he had his cigarette going, he said, "When she was told her husband was dead — *really* dead this time — she went crazy. She was like a madwoman. She screamed vitriolic threats against everyone, particularly you and *Monsieur* Graylock and me. It took several people to hold her. Then she collapsed and began to babble incoherently. After that she began to talk more rationally and, with a little urging from the police, confessed everything. It was she and her husband who had made Janine take Gloria's baby to the orphanage. They did not quite dare to kill it at that time. Their plan was to incapacitate Gloria, with the aid of her father and the various drugs they fed her. Then, when that was accomplished and her father had gained control of her money, they would do away with him. And Veronica, as his only relative, would inherit everything."

I almost choked on my brandy. "You mean Mr. Graylock knew about Baron von Meyerhoff?"

"No. Aunt Veronica had managed to contact him wherever he was in Italy, and when Graylock bought my château, she smuggled him in. *Madame Fouchette* was in league with her, and old *Philippe*. There was much money changing hands. And some of the people who rented the château during these last three years were friends of Aunt Veronica's and the Baron's. They helped Meyerhoff to set up a laboratory in the closed off part of the château, on the top floor. There he has been experimenting with drugs and various forms of the laser ray, one of which was the laser ray knife which, when perfected, will be a boon to surgeons. Unfortunately, he took advantage of his knowledge, and since Gloria arrived here this time, he experimented on her with his new drugs." He sighed. "Poor girl, she didn't have a chance against them."

"And Janine?"

"After Gloria came back, Janine threatened to tell about the baby. Naturally, they couldn't allow that. So one night, while she was sleeping, Meyerhoff chloroformed her, took her up to the laboratory, slit her throat, then took her down and left her in the courtyard to die."

I shuddered, and Paul poured me a little more brandy. "What will they do with Aunt Veronica?"

"I do not know. But now she has confessed about my son, I will be able to get him quite soon."

"Oh, Paul!" I cried. "I am so glad!"

He disposed of his cigarette and took my brandy glass away from me so he could take me in his arms. "I will need your help, Carol," he said. "You will have to marry me and be a mother to little Paul."

I looked up into his earnest, beautiful gray eyes and, holding my lips close to his, asked, "Is that the only reason you want me?"

His arms tightened around me, and he began to breathe faster. Against me I could feel his heart beating faster and faster, as my own was doing. "You know better than that," he said. "I love you. *Je t'adore*. Oh, my darling! *Ma chérie!*" Then our lips were together; pressing, pressing, parting. We clung to each other as if we would never let one another go.

Then the doors of the drawing room opened, and Celeste said, *"Pardon, monsieur dame,* but the *gendarmes,* they are very persistent. They want to talk to you. And the reporters have come over from *Nice."*

Paul and I separated, and Paul nodded and stood up. "I will talk to them," he said wearily. "You stay here with *mademoiselle."*

Celeste smiled and came and sat down beside me. "I am so glad for you, *mademoiselle,*" she said, color returning to her cheeks and her dark eyes sparkling. "He is the *perfect* man, *Monsieur Paul.* The absolutely *perfect man!"*

I couldn't help smiling. "I thoroughly agree with you," I said.

Then she asked, "The little one — you have seen him?"

I said, "Yes. He is the image of his father."

Celeste nodded. "He would be. The Thireau men, they all look alike."

Chapter Fifteen

For what was left of the night, Paul took Celeste and me down to his villa. It seems Celeste and Marie are distantly related, so they were happy to see each other and were chaperones for me. The next day I moved to a small hotel in Nice to await whatever the future held in store for Paul and me.

Mr. Graylock and Mark arrived two days after the tragedies, but they did not stay long. Gloria was cremated and her ashes taken back to be buried beside her mother on Long Island. Baron von Meyerhoff's body was kept in the morgue at Nice until the newspaper publicity on the case flushed out some of his friends, who had rented the château at one time. Then they took him back to Germany.

I saw Mark only once while he was in France. He came to see me at my hotel in Nice. He was a very subdued Mark. He said, among other things, "I suppose it is too late for us to pick up the pieces?"

I said, "Much too late. I am going to marry Paul Thireau."

"I wish you wouldn't."

"Nothing could change my mind. I love him very dearly."

We were in the little sitting room that opened off the lobby of the small hotel. He kept his eyes on my face. They reminded me of a cocker spaniel pleading for understanding. He said, "I am resigning from the agency. I couldn't bear to stay there."

I said, "I am sorry things turned out this way for you."

He shrugged. "When all this mess gets into the New York papers and on radio and TV, I doubt if the Graylock Agency will be able to continue. I don't know if what Graylock has done to his stepdaughter can be called a criminal offense, but whether it is or not, he is through. And if any of Gloria's money comes to me, I shall give it to her son. I couldn't touch it."

I asked, "When you married Gloria, didn't you suspect about the pills?"

"No. I thought she was acting strangely because she didn't want to be bothered with me. I guess I was a fool. I should have suspected during the two weeks I was with her at the château. But — well, every time I tried to make love to her, she would push me away. And she wouldn't let me sleep in her room. I had a room down the hall, opposite Aunt Veronica's."

I said, "She didn't really have anything against you, Mark. She was still in love with Paul."

He got up and walked out into the lobby, and I followed him. At the entrance, he looked down at me lingeringly. "Could I kiss you goodbye?"

"I'd rather you didn't."

He sighed. "Well, I can't blame you. Goodbye, Carol. And I hope you and Paul will be happy."

"Thank you. I'm sure we will be. And goodbye, Mark. Good luck." He walked out of the hotel and got into a taxi. That was the last I saw of him.

Mr. Graylock kept away from me, for which I was glad. After he returned to New York, he mailed me a sizable check, which I returned without even a thank you.

So far, Aunt Veronica has not recovered from the shock of her husband's death and the failure of her carefully laid plans. She was eventually transferred to a mental hospital, where she will probably live out her life, what is left of it.

Mr. Graylock, faced with the disgrace, shame and tragedy of what had happened to his stepdaughter, and the knowledge that his beloved sister had planned to kill him, together with the loss of his business, died of a heart attack a few weeks later. At least it was reported as a heart attack. There were some who thought he had taken an overdose of the pills he had fed his stepdaughter.

No one in any of the pharmaceutical houses would admit having given any kind of pills to him at any time, and it was thought he must have gotten them from various drug peddlers in the city.

It was about six weeks before Paul was able to get little Paul, and by that time the child, as Mr.

Graylock's and Gloria's only heir, had inherited all the money that had caused the trouble in the first place. He also inherited the château, which is being kept closed until he is of age and knows what he wants to do with it.

Madame Fouchette and *Philippe* were let go when the château was closed up, but Paul and I are keeping *Celeste* and *Jacques* with us, to help Marie, who is going to have her hands full with the added work I and little Paul will make for her.

Paul and I were married in Nice the week before little Paul came home to live with us, and we had a short honeymoon along the French and Italian Riviera. It was heavenly.

One day, toward the end of the summer, Paul, little Paul and I were having lunch on the terrace by the garden of the villa when little Paul asked us, "Are you always going to be my mummy and daddy?"

Simultaneously we said, "Always," and each took one of his chubby little hands.

He smiled and looked from one to the other. "I'm glad," he said. "I like you."

Without meeting Paul's eyes, I asked the child, "Would you like to have a little sister or maybe a little brother to play with?"

He smiled, and his gray eyes, so like Paul's, shone with happiness as he nodded his head eagerly.

I won't tell you what big Paul said.

The employees of G.K. Hall hope you have enjoyed this Large Print book. All our Large Print titles are designed for easy reading, and all our books are made to last. Other G.K. Hall books are available at your library, through selected bookstores, or directly from us.

For information about titles, please call:

(800) 257-5157

To share your comments, please write:

Publisher
G.K. Hall & Co.
P.O. Box 159
Thorndike, ME 04986